CHALLENGING DANTE

CHALLENGING DANTE

BY
LYNNE GRAHAM

Published in Great Britain 2013
by Mills & Boon, an imprint of Harlequin (UK) Limited.
Large Print edition 2014
Harlequin (UK) Limited, Eton House,
18-24 Paradise Road, Richmond, Surrey, TW9 1SR

© 2013 Lynne Graham

ISBN: 978 0 263 24004 7

9780263240047

CO 15363797

Printed and bound in Great Britain
by CPI Antony Rowe, Chippenham, Wiltshire

CHAPTER ONE

DANTE LEONETTI, INTERNATIONAL BANKER, renowned philanthropist and the Conte di Martino to those whom such archaic titles mattered, frowned at the news that his childhood friend, Marco Savonelli, was outside his office waiting to see him. Something *had* to be seriously wrong to drag Marco from his village doctor's surgery all the way to the fast-moving financial centre of Milan.

Lean, darkly handsome features composed in a frown, Dante pushed long brown fingers through his luxuriant black hair in a gesture of concern rare for a man with his tough, self-disciplined temperament. Surely Marco's visit could only be related to the fund? Between them the two men were engaged in raising money by a variety of means to finance pioneering medical treatment in the USA for a village child stricken with leukaemia. From the outset, Dante had offered to cover the entire cost of the venture but Marco had persuaded him that it would be much more diplomatic to allow the village community as a whole to assume responsibility and volunteer their services to raise the thousands of euros required. Various public events had accordingly been organised and a fancy-dress ball at Dante's family home, the Castello Leonetti in Tuscany, was the next big date and indeed the grand finale on the calendar, Dante recalled grimly, for he would have preferred to make a huge donation rather than be forced to dress up in comical clothes like a child at play. He had no patience for such nonsense.

His phone pinged and although he sighed he was conditioned by years as a banker to always be on the alert. But the message was not from one of his aides warning him of some potential crisis. It was from his mistress, the beautiful Della, and he frowned down at the picture of her superb breasts, his handsome mouth curling with irritation as he deleted the shot with an impatient stab. He didn't want dirty pictures on his mobile; he was *not* a teenage boy, he reflected grimly. Clearly it was time to give Della the proverbial golden handshake and make a smooth exit. Unhappily the prospect of pastures new to explore held no attraction for him yet he knew he was bored with Della and even more bored with her colossal vanity and her avarice.

Yet, genuine warmth filled Dante's uncommon green eyes when he crossed his big office to greet Marco Savonelli, a stockily built male in his early thirties, and the exact opposite of Dante in temperament for cheerful Marco was rarely seen without a smile on his face. Well, just this once his friend wasn't smiling, Dante noted. Indeed Marco's expressive face was unusually tense and troubled.

'I'm really sorry to disturb you like this,' Marco began awkwardly, very much a fish out of water as he took in the opulence of his surroundings. 'I didn't want to bother you—'

'Relax, Marco. Take a seat and we'll have coffee,' Dante advised, urging his old friend in the direction of the luxurious seating area.

'I had no idea how fancy your place of work would be,' the other man confided ruefully. 'To think that I thought I'd reached the height of sophistication when the practice manager installed my computer...'

The coffee arrived at lightning speed. 'It's not like you to take time out from your patients,' Dante remarked, eager for Marco to tell him exactly what was wrong. 'Has someone embezzled money from the fund, something of that nature?'

Marco, evidently very much more innocent than Dante had ever been, shot him a look of horror. 'Of course not! It's nothing to do with the fund and...er...actually, I was coming to Milan anyway to visit my aunt Serafina on my mother's behalf, so I thought I would just drop in and see how you were while I was in the neighbourhood.'

Dante, sharp as a tack when it came to reading people, recognised a cover story coming his way and marvelled that Marco believed that he could fool someone as astute as he was. 'Is that so?'

'And as I said since I'm here anyway,' Marco continued, gathering speed like a reluctant man pushing himself towards something he would rather have avoided, 'I saw no harm in calling in for a chat.'

Trying not to laugh at his old friend's transparency, Dante murmured lazily, 'Why not?'

'Have you heard much from your mother recently?'

Dante froze, his keen intelligence taking his thoughts in a different direction. 'She phones and chats most days,' he responded with studied casualness, long black lashes dropping low in concealment over his shrewd gaze as, for the first time, honest tension clenched his big, well-built body.

'Oh, is that so? Good…er…excellent…' Marco countered, visibly not having expected to receive so reassuring a reply. 'But when did you last visit?'

Dante stiffened, wondering if that was a hint

of censure. 'I assumed the newly-weds would prefer to be left in peace.'

'Of course…of course,' Marco hastened to reassure him in a tone of apology. 'A natural assumption even at their age. And…er…forgive me if I cause offence, although you have never said anything on the score of your mother's re-marriage, it must have come as a surprise to you.'

As he recognised that he might well still be waiting for his overly tactful friend to get to the point in another hour, Dante suppressed his innate desire to keep his every feeling and reaction private and decided to be blunt. 'More than a surprise,' he admitted flatly. 'I was shocked and worried by it. Not only was my mother's decision to remarry very sudden but I was also dismayed by her choice of husband.'

'Yet you said nothing at the time,' Marco groaned. 'If only you could have been more plainspoken with me, Dante.'

'My mother led a wretched life with my late father for more years than I care to recall. He was a bastard. That is not something I would acknowledge to anyone but you. Bearing that in mind, I am the last man alive likely to criticise her bridegroom or interfere in her attempt to, at long last, find a little happiness.'

Sympathy now etched in his kindly brown eyes, Marco visibly relaxed. 'I can understand that.'

A brooding expression on his lean features, Dante was recalling his widowed mother's sudden marriage to Vittore Ravallo. The wedding had taken place only two months earlier. Ravallo was a failed businessman and onetime womaniser, who was as poor as Sofia, Contessa di Martino, was rich. The marriage had been impulsive and improvident but Dante was a loyal and loving son and he had kept his reservations to himself. If need be he would intervene to protect his mother should the marriage prove to be the mistake he assumed it was, but in the short term he would mind his own business. Even so, that considerate restraint had proved a challenge, particularly when the happy couple was still oc-

cupying Dante's castle in Tuscany while they
waited for renovations to be completed on their
new home several miles away. For that reason,
Dante had not been back to *Castello Leonetti* for
a visit since the small private wedding that had
sealed his mother's fate.

Marco compressed his mouth. 'Perhaps you
could consider going home soon. There's something strange going on.'

Dante almost laughed out loud at that statement. *'Strange?'*

'I've never been a man to listen to gossip but
we've been friends all our lives and I felt I should
give you a hint about what has been happening.'

'So...' Dante summed up rather drily, not interested in his friend's penchant for drama, 'what
is happening at the castle, Marco?'

'Well, you know what an energetic woman
your mother has always been?' Marco remarked.
'Not any more. She's no longer involved in her
usual charitable pursuits either, never leaves the
castle and no longer even gardens.'

Dante frowned, unable to even imagine his

very active mother suddenly abandoning the busy life she had built as widow to that extent. 'That does sound strange...'

'And then there's her new social secretary—'

'Her...*what*?' Dante cut in, taken aback. 'She's hired a secretary?'

'A young English girl, very attractive and apparently perfectly pleasant,' Marco recounted uncomfortably. 'But now she's standing in for the contessa at her charitable engagements and she's often been seen getting lifts from Vittore—'

Dante was very still, an attitude that his employees knew as the calm before the storm, for the inclusion of a young and attractive girl in the set-up that Marco was describing had him seething with anger. Many older men were fools when it came to young girls and Dante's stepfather might very well be one of them. His heart sank on his mother's behalf. He had hoped that if the marriage failed it would do so on less wounding grounds for his parent than that of another woman. His own father's infidelity had already caused Sofia Leonetti so much pain that Dante simply could not stand by and watch it happen again.

'*Is* there an affair going on?' Dante demanded, hands clenching into fists by his side as he sprang upright, unable to stay seated any longer.

'I honestly don't know. There's no evidence of one, nothing more suspect than the look of things,' Marco responded ruefully. 'And we all know how misleading appearances can sometimes be. But there is one odd aspect to that girl that doesn't quite add up—'

'Go on,' Dante urged in a raw undertone, struggling with his outrage at the image of his mother being humiliatingly betrayed by an employee and her new husband in his home.

'My father was invited to a dinner at the castle for Vittore's birthday. The girl was wearing a diamond necklace that my father swore is worth many, many thousands of euros.'

And both men were well aware that Marco's father was an infallible judge of such things because he was a renowned jewellery designer.

'Of course it *could* be a family heirloom,' Marco conceded fairly.

'But how likely is it that a young office worker would own such an item or even bring it abroad with her?' Dante retorted, unimpressed by that argument. 'As far as I'm concerned, when you take everything else into account, the diamonds are hard evidence of misbehaviour of some kind!'

But even if it was, what the hell was he planning to do about it? Dante asked himself angrily after his friend had taken his leave. Obviously Dante would go home to personally check out the situation and if there was anything questionable afoot *he* would deal with the girl with the diamond necklace.

Topsy suppressed a groan of frustration as her sister Kat continued to challenge her with worried questions on the phone. What were the family she was living with like? Were there any men coming on to her? Did she have a lock on her bedroom door?

The guilt that Topsy had initially experienced about lying to her family about what she was doing and where she was staying in Italy suddenly dissipated like a damp squib. What age did her big sister think she was? A vulnerable teenager? For goodness' sake, she was almost twenty-four years old with a doctorate in advanced maths, scarcely a babe in arms! But Kat, just like Topsy's twin older sisters, Emmie and Saffy, simply refused to accept that Topsy had grown up and had a life of her own to lead.

In Kat's defence, she *had* been acting more as Topsy's mother than her sister since Topsy was six years old and the sisters' birth mother, Odette, stuck all three of her younger children in foster care so that she could reclaim her freedom as a single woman. No, Odette Taylor had had no taste for mothering and Topsy was all too well aware of how much she and her sisters owed Kat for her loving care and loyalty. Kat had taken custody of her younger siblings, whisked them off to her home in the Lake District and raised them to adulthood at her own expense.

Kat's sacrifice could never be forgotten or go unappreciated, Topsy acknowledged ruefully.

Yet here she was in Italy having run away from home and lied about her whereabouts just like the teenager she had long since left behind! Her family thought she was simply enjoying an extended break staying with an old school friend and Gabrielle was happy to provide the cover story and pretend—should she ever be challenged—that Topsy was living with her and her family in Milan.

Topsy sighed, guilt licking at her conscience again. Her siblings were so overprotective they regularly drove her to screaming point. Their marriages to rich and powerful men had only enhanced their desire and ability to interfere and control Topsy's every move. She loved them, she truly did, indeed she *adored* her sisters and their closeness, but she didn't want a job doled out by one of their husbands and she didn't want to be landed with a pre-checked boyfriend either. She had lost count of the eligible and no doubt thoroughly vetted men produced for her benefit at parties and dinners. She had also lost count of the boyfriends she had lost, who had failed to pass the family vetting procedure. In addition the insistence on her, at one unforgettably embarrassing stage, having a bodyguard had done nothing to advance her prospects in the romantic stakes.

Either men wanted her purely because of her wealthy brothers-in-laws' financial and business connections or all the hoopla of even dating her frightened them off. Even worse, she was now a trust-fund baby, gifted with a sizeable amount of cash on her twenty-first birthday in a generous group gift from her sisters' husbands, so that she would always be independent and secure. *Independent?* Topsy grimaced at a goal long craved but always out of reach. What a joke the concept of independence was! That wretched money, which she had never wanted but which had delighted her anxious and overprotective sisters, had only trapped her more than ever in a world in which she didn't feel she belonged. Now her sisters' husbands would only have an even better excuse to check out any man she dated for fear he might be after her trust fund!

But then that wasn't the *only* reason Topsy had come to Italy and to this particular household in Tuscany, she conceded sheepishly. Indeed if any member of her family were to discover the true nature of the deception she was engaged in, they would be justifiably furious with her. None of them would understand, she thought sadly, none of them would ever appreciate how powerful a motivation she had had to come to Italy and pretend to be something she was not. But then she was not the same as her sisters: their outlook on certain issues was directly opposed to hers. Right and wrong were not as black and white as they believed, she reasoned uncomfortably. Of course some day if things went as she hoped she would have to tell them the truth. Right now she was at the awkward dishonest outset of her mission and the false image she had set up was already discomfiting her. Before her arrival in Italy, Topsy had virtually never told a lie. She had been a squeaky clean and very logical child who recognised at an early age the inherent consequences of lies. Yet here she was all these years on and supposedly intelligent and mature and she was lying her head off all around her! And to such lovely people too, she reflected even more painfully. Why was it that the drawbacks of her mission had only occurred to her *after* she had taken up residence and started work? How was that for poor forward planning?

Yet how could she simply give up a cause that meant so much to her? Her sisters though would never understand that angle: they would simply fiercely disapprove. And if they knew the lengths her mother had forced her to go to before she would finally divulge the information that Topsy craved, they would have been outraged, Topsy conceded heavily. But in her opinion, it had been worth it to finally get the truth... if it *was* the truth. Unfortunately she was all too well aware she could not totally trust her mother's word.

Meanwhile she was living in the lap of luxury

in a genuine medieval castle, which had been owned by the Leonetti family for hundreds of years. Yet her beautiful surroundings had that wonderful lived-in vibe, which made even the splendid furnishings emanate a warm and cosy ambience. No, she certainly couldn't complain about the standard of her living conditions.

Mid-morning the next day, her dark eyes shadowed by a restless night of troubled thoughts, Topsy was in the garden cutting roses for the contessa to arrange. The superb rose garden basked in the heat of the sun shining down from the clear blue sky above and it was so warm that Topsy was relieved she was only wearing a cool cotton skirt and tee shirt. Vittore, who generally got involved in anything relating to his only recently acquired wife, crossed the bed of roses to extend a particularly lovely rich pink bloom to her. 'It's La Noblesse…her favourite,' he explained, a small, slightly built man in his late forties with benevolent dark eyes and a still-handsome face.

'You're identifying them now?' Topsy teased even though she was touched by his consideration for Sofia. 'Your time with that rose book is certainly paying off!'

Vittore laughed, turned a little red and smiled warmly.

This was the little tableau that Dante was deeply disturbed to witness as he strode round the corner of the castle to access the side entrance. Like a pantomime lech, his grinning stepfather was extending a rose to a giggling young brunette. Even if Marco hadn't planted suspicion in Dante's mind he would have become suspicious at the sight of such conspicuous familiarity between an older man and a youthful employee.

'Vittore...' Dante breathed, quietly announcing his presence.

Startled, his stepfather whirled round so fast he almost fell over a shrub and, righting himself, stiffened and froze in place still standing in the rose bed. 'Dante,' he acknowledged with a

rather forced smile. 'This is Topsy. She's working here to help your mother with her charities.'

Topsy stared at the tall black-haired male who
had appeared out of nowhere. So, this was Dante,
Sofia's beloved only child, the selfish, unfeeling
cad, who had spoiled the older couple's wedding with his cold attitude and even quicker departure. Of course she had seen a photo of him
in Sofia's sitting room but no two-dimensional
image could possibly have conveyed the devas-
tating effect of Dante Leonetti in the flesh.

He was drop-dead gorgeous from the crown
of his luxuriant black hair to the soles of his undoubtedly handmade shoes. His dark suit said
he meant business and was faultlessly tailored to
his lean powerful frame. He stalked closer like a
predator closing in on its prey and she blinked,
wondering where that strange comparison had
come from. Within six feet of them he came to
a halt and the sheer height and breadth of him
intimidated her, reminding her of the undeni-
able drawbacks of being just four feet ten and
a half inches tall. His extraordinary eyes made

her stare for they were an unexpectedly exquisite shade of green, strikingly luminous and light against his bronzed skin and oddly unsettling. An unfamiliar sense of breathlessness afflicted her.

Her body felt weirdly detached from her brain while a series of bizarre reactions was filtering through her. All of a sudden, her breasts felt incredibly sensitive and an uncomfortable clenching sensation between her legs made her instinctively press her thighs together. Sexual attraction? She refused to believe that it could be. She couldn't possibly be attracted to a male she was already programmed to thoroughly dislike!

Dante studied the tiny brunette with fierce attention. Her glossy mane of curling dark hair fell down her back almost to her waist. She had wide almond-shaped eyes the colour of melted honey, creamy olive skin and a ripe pink mouth. Her beautiful face was the shape of a heart and, for all her surprising lack of height, she had the pronounced curves of a pocket Venus. The ripe swell of her full breasts pushed against her thin cotton top while the opulent flare of the hips below her tiny waist was neatly delineated by the fitted skirt. Dante was startled by the instantaneous swelling sensation at his groin for not since he was an undisciplined teenager had he reacted that strongly at first sight of a woman. Annoyingly, she wasn't even his type, she absolutely *wasn't* his type: he went for tall elegant blondes and always had. But evidently his treacherous hormones had a different opinion and he had cause to be grateful for the suit jacket he still wore.

Topsy extended a slim hand. 'Topsy Marshall.'

'Dante Leonetti,' Dante told her as he grasped her small hand, barely aware of his stepfather still hovering in the background while his keen scrutiny remained welded to Topsy's smiling face.

His brain kicked back into gear. Of course she was smiling at him, of course she was responding with charm! How else would she treat a very rich man? After all, if she was a gold-digger, he was a wealthier and much more rewarding target than Vittore could ever be. On the back of that thought the germ of an excellent idea flared through Dante. He was rich and single and consequently had to be a much more tempting prospect than his stepfather. Possibly, Vittore was still only flirting with the idea of adultery, for Dante was convinced that Vittore would not be going to the idiotic lengths of gathering roses if he had already got into the little brunette's bed. Surmising that nothing very much had yet happened between the couple, Dante recognised that *he* had the power to nip the relationship in the bud and protect his mother in the short term. If *he* showed an interest in his mother's employee, Vittore would have to master his weakness and back off.

'Your mother will be eager to see you,' Topsy remarked.

Her use of fluent Italian surprised Dante. 'You speak our language?'

'I speak several languages,' Topsy admitted lightly. 'But my best friend at school was Italian and we shared a room, so I picked up more colloquial phrases.'

'You have a commendable grasp,' Dante remarked, curious about her for the first time. 'What other languages do you speak?'

'French, Spanish and German. Rather old-fashioned choices,' Topsy commented wryly. 'I wish I'd had the foresight to study Russian and Chinese. Even a working knowledge of those might have been more useful.'

Dante shrugged a broad shoulder as he moved towards the entrance. 'You can't lose with those languages while you're living in Europe.'

'I'll take you straight up to see your mother,' Vittore volunteered, hurrying towards the stone staircase at the rear of the hall.

'And I must deliver the roses before they start to wilt,' Topsy added, her heart beating very fast as Dante momentarily paused to shoot a razor-edged glance at her that was anything but friendly. What on earth was wrong with the man? Had he disliked her on sight?

Dante ground his even white teeth together.

He was in his own home and he had not seen his mother for weeks. He needed neither a guide to her rooms nor companions and was immediately suspicious. Vittore slung him an almost apprehensive look over his shoulder as he reached the top of the stairs, his attention shooting anxiously to Topsy. Witnessing that revealing byplay between them, Dante sensed a powerful hint of duplicity that put him even more on his guard.

The contessa smiled warmly as her husband entered her charming private sitting room.

'I have a surprise for you,' Vittore said tautly.

And then, a split second later, as Dante strode through the door the small slim brunette, who had been reclining on the comfortable chaise longue by the window flew to her feet and cried, 'Dante! Why didn't you tell me you were coming?'

'I was scared I would be forced to cancel at the last moment.' Dante kissed his mother's cheek and then grasped her hands to stand back and look at her. 'You look pale, tired—'

Recognising the flicker of dismay in the older

woman's eyes at that remark, Topsy spoke up before she could think better of it. 'Your mother's
still recovering from the bout of flu she had a
couple of weeks ago.'

'Yes…it took a lot out of me,' Sofia confirmed
the lie while sending Topsy a warm glance for
providing her with that easy excuse. 'Come and
sit down, Topsy—'

'I think I should get on with some work,' Topsy
protested as Sofia settled back down onto the
chaise longue and patted the space beside her.
In her late forties, Sofia was still a very pretty
woman with the same unusual clear green eyes
that distinguished her son.

'No, no,' Vittore argued, reaching for the house
phone with alacrity. 'Take a break. I'll order coffee for us.'

Dante watched in silence while Topsy took
a seat beside his mother, his handsome mouth
compressing with disapproval as he recognised
that the older woman was treating the girl more
like a favoured niece than an employee. Quite
clearly she had no suspicions whatsoever about

the younger woman's character or, indeed, her behaviour with her husband. Vittore, meanwhile, hovered beside the chaise longue within reach of his wife, the very epitome of the devoted husband he wanted Dante to believe he was.

In reaction, hostility flared through Dante's lean, powerful frame and he wondered if anger was making him paranoid for, observing the cosy little threesome, he was convinced he was being treated to an act designed to pull the wool over his eyes. Yet what could his mother possibly have to hide from him? Sofia and her son had always been close. His reading of the situation, his conviction that something was badly amiss, *had* to be wrong, he reasoned in growing frustration.

CHAPTER TWO

Topsy GOT UP and walked through to the adjoining cloakroom to put the cut roses in water and then she answered the knock on the door that preceded the housekeeper, Carmela's entrance with a tray of coffee and cakes. The grey-haired older woman reacted to Dante as though he were the prodigal son with a fatted calf to be slaughtered to celebrate his return.

Topsy returned to her seat while Vittore arranged a table beside his wife so that she could pour the coffee. While that was going on, Topsy studied Dante. Those eyes, fringed by long black lashes in that lean dark face were utterly stunning, she conceded grudgingly, unsettled that such a thought should even occur to her for he was not the type of man who should ever appeal to her. He wore his elegant business suit like a second skin and his sleek aura of well-groomed arrogance and command reminded her strongly of her bossy brothers-in-law. Dante Leonetti, she reflected abstractedly, would have all the imagination of a stone and would only think in terms of power and profit. Money was all important to him and undoubtedly the yardstick by which he judged other men. She suspected that had Vittore Ravallo been a rich and powerful man, Dante might well have welcomed him into the family.

How could anyone dislike someone as sweet and inoffensive as Vittore? Even so, although Dante might be offensive he was still, indisputably, a stunningly beautiful man. The shock of that second disturbing acknowledgement almost floored Topsy where she sat, for she had never been the susceptible sort, impressed by outward appearance. After all, her sisters were married to handsome men and she was accustomed to their looks. But no matter how hard she tried to concentrate on something else her attention remained hopelessly locked to Dante, noting the arrow-straight flare of his nose, the level black brows, the spectacular bone structure and the strong stubborn jaw line already darkening with stubble. She shifted uneasily where she sat, shocked by the sensations flooding her treacherous body and appalled to realise that for the first time in her life she was greedily wondering if a man would look as good naked as he did clothed. Her lashes fluttered as she tried to suppress that embarrassingly intimate thought while still guiltily engaged in mentally mapping the impressive breadth of his shoulders, the muscular width of the chest flexing beneath his silk shirt and the neat fit of his expensive trousers pulled taut over his long, powerful thighs.

Dante's handsome dark head whipped round and he met her wide dark gaze in a head-on collision. Topsy felt her face flame red as fire, mortification claiming her entire body in a scorching blush as she literally tore her scrutiny from him, lowering her head as awkward as a schoolgirl caught out, only to find that her wretched gaze accidentally fell on the very last part of him she should be studying: the prominent masculine bulge at his crotch. It was as if Dante Leonetti put out sexual pheromones that fried her brain cells and all she could think about was touching him, tracing that arrogant blade of a nose, caressing that roughened jaw line, smoothing hands in worshipping exploration of places she had never touched before but longed to discover.

'Excuse me...' Dante sprang upright and strode over to the window, turning his back to them and thrusting the latch open to filter in fresh air to the stuffy room. *Madre di Dio...* He had never known temptation could come in such a small unexpected package, had never dreamt that involuntary arousal could seize him when he was in every way an adult in full control of his libido. What the hell was happening to him? Why was Topsy Marshall having this effect on him? It was not as though he were sex-starved or had even had much interest in that direction of recent. He ground his perfect white teeth together in bemused frustration, striving not to picture the diamond-hard pointed buttons of her nipples indenting her tee shirt, the mere hint of a shadowy vee between her creamy thighs as the hem of her skirt rode up. It was like being shot back screaming to the teen years when his control over his own body had been a bad joke. So exactly what was it about her that got to him? A tiny, shapely brunette, years his junior, not a raving beauty by any means but sexy, impossibly, *outrageously* sexy.

'Are you feeling all right, Dante?' his mother asked curiously.

'I was too warm,' Dante murmured flatly. 'Would you mind if I took a run over to see how the work is progressing on your house? I feel like some fresh air.'

'Of course I wouldn't mind and if you don't mind taking Topsy with you, Vittore and I will be able to have lunch together,' his mother remarked. 'Topsy has to see my decorator and check that he's redone the kitchen the way I wanted it. I don't know what I would have done without her help. For a while there, I had far too much on my plate.'

Dante skimmed a glance in Topsy's direction

that didn't linger. 'We'll go as soon as we've had our coffee.'

Not best pleased by the news that she would be visiting the Casa di Fortuna in Dante's company rather than Vittore's, Topsy had stiffened, gripped by the most maddening self-consciousness she had ever experienced. She was afraid to look near the wretched man in case he cast a spell over her again. She wasn't stupid: she knew she was attracted to him and that it was a stronger attraction than she had ever felt before. So superficial of her too, she scolded herself wryly, being physically drawn to a male who was a virtual stranger and with whom she would not have a thought or feeling in common. It was yet another complexity in her life that she really didn't need, but hopefully he was only making a fleeting visit to the castle to see his mother. From what she understood, Dante spent little time in his Tuscan home and much preferred the faster, more sophisticated pace of Milan.

She listened quietly while her companions made polite conversation, Sofia mentioning recent visitors and small domestic concerns at the castle while parrying her son's concerned questions about her mythical bout of influenza. *Oh what a tangled web we weave when first we practise to deceive!* Sir Walter Scott's words were as relevant to Vittore and Sofia as to Topsy. They all had their secrets from which Dante was being excluded but, watching the frown slowly darkening Dante's face, she reckoned he was fully aware of the covert undertones.

Why, oh, why had she walked into the lion's den without thought of what *her* secret might cost others? Self-loathing momentarily gripped Topsy. Her twin sisters had got by fine being ignored by their father after their parents divorced and their father remarried. Topsy's father had not married her mother but she was still desperate to know *who* he was. Perhaps that very desperation was driven by the fact that for most of her life she had mistakenly believed that she did know who had fathered her: a handsome South American polo player called Paolo Valdera, who had enjoyed a brief affair with her mother. After all, over the years she had met Paolo several times when he visited London and there had been the occasional phone call around Christmas or her birthday. Sadly, although Paolo had apparently accepted without question that he was Topsy's father, he had been very little more interested in his supposed daughter than her mother had been.

Then when she was eighteen Paolo had discovered that he was sterile and had finally asked for DNA testing, the results of which had proved that he could not possibly be Topsy's dad. Topsy had had to go to great lengths to get another name out of her mother and the only name she had been given was Vittore's.

Getting close to Vittore and working out exactly what kind of a man he was had been Topsy's main motivation in applying for the job working for Sofia. She had been driven by entirely selfish promptings, never pausing to consider that such a bombshell as the existence of an adult illegitimate daughter could damage his very new and happy marriage. For that reason, while she had learned to like Vittore Ravallo, she had done nothing to check out her mother's story and could not even begin to imagine asking Vittore to subject himself to DNA tests to satisfy her craving to know who she was. Right now, Vittore had far more pressing concerns on his mind and Topsy was very unwilling to do or say anything that might risk upsetting Dante's mother.

Dante rose to his full height, fluid as quicksilver for all his size. 'We'll leave now.'

'Don't pass the work that's been done in the kitchen unless it's perfect,' Sofia warned her firmly.

'Why don't you accompany us?' Dante asked lightly.

His mother tensed. 'I hate the smell of paint.'

Sofia also got horribly car sick, Topsy conceded, happy to stand in for the older woman if it helped her to rest and regain her strength. Struggling to keep up with Dante's long impatient stride, she accompanied him downstairs and out to the rear of the castle where one of the collection of high-powered cars he owned had already been extracted for his benefit from the garage block. It was a Pagani Zonda. Saffy's husband, Zahir, owned one of these high-powered sports cars although as the king of the Arabian Gulf state of Maraban he never seemed to get the opportunity to drive himself anywhere. Boys and their toys, she thought wryly.

'Nice wheels,' she said, reckoning it was another nail in the coffin of her attraction to him, another reminder that they would be a poor match in every way. The gilded extras of life did not impress her although she would have been the first to admit that since Kat had assumed charge of her as a child she had never known what it was to want for anything she needed. In so many ways she had been spoiled as the baby of the family and perhaps that was why she had had to run away to grow up.

'I gather Vittore drives you around quite a lot,' Dante commented as she slid in beside him.

'I need lifts anywhere I can't walk or ride a bike,' Topsy admitted. 'I can't drive.'

Dante frowned, his surprise unconcealed. 'That must make doing the job a challenge.'

'Yes,' Topsy conceded, since it was the truth, watching a lean brown hand glide smoothly round the steering wheel, angling the powerful car through the castle gates and down through the village beyond the ancient estate walls. 'But neither your mother nor I thought of the need for me to drive during our interview.'

'You could learn. I'll fix the paperwork,' Dante informed her.

'I've failed the driving test a few times at home...I don't really want to try again,' Topsy said truthfully.

'How many times?' Dante asked.

Topsy stiffened. 'Six times. That was enough for me. I've got poor co-ordination and lousy spatial awareness. Everyone's got a weakness—that's mine and I can live with it.'

'Any idiot can drive,' Dante retorted, unimpressed, seeing how she could be detached from Vittore in one way at least. 'I'll teach you while I'm here.'

Topsy winced at the prospect. 'Thanks but no, thanks.'

'It wasn't a suggestion, it was an order,' Dante told her lethally. 'To fully perform your duties, you should be able to drive.'

Topsy stared straight out of the windscreen at the magnificent scenery as the car descended the hill into the rolling valley studded with shapely cypresses and the serrated green lines of the vineyards, her expressive mouth silently forming a rude word of disagreement. 'I work for your mother, not for you. I don't have to do what you tell me to do.'

His long fingers flexed expressively round the steering wheel and she stole a reluctant glance at him, noting the taut set of his bold bronzed profile while she doubted that he met in-your-face rebellion very often from subordinates. Momentarily, his shimmering green gaze flared in her direction and a crackling energy filled the atmosphere with tension. Topsy breathed in deep and slow, smoothed her skirt down over her slim thighs and tactfully said nothing.

'So, tell me what qualified you for the job,' Dante invited without skipping a beat.

Topsy was more intimidated by his self-discipline than she would have been had he snapped angrily back at her. 'I have a lot of experience with charity committee work, volunteers and functions,' she confided, recalling the long educational summer stays in Maraban while her sister Saffy concentrated her time on benevolent good works as befitted the wife of a ruler, not to mention her sister Kat's ventures in the same line. 'I also speak the language and I'm very versatile and not too proud to do whatever needs to be done. Basically I'm your mother's gopher. I deal with all the decorating hassles at the new house as well. Your mother has a very clear picture of how she wants every room to look. I'm also handling the arrangements for the fancy-dress ball.'

His jaw line set granite hard. 'Try to understand my surprise at your employment. My mother has never required assistance before.'

'But then she had made her charities and your

very extensive gardens into a full-time job,' Topsy pointed out a shade drily. 'And now the contessa wants the time to relax and be with her husband. She's also hired another full-time gardener to help out on the estate.'

If possible, Dante's stubborn chin and firm mouth took on an even more hostile set. 'I know my mother.'

No, you don't, Topsy thought silently. He was out of the inner circle now and evidently not yet to be trusted with the news that had torn Sofia's neat and tidy life apart. Really, that aspect was none of her business either but she had no intention of betraying the contessa's trust. Sofia had been very kind to Topsy and she was determined to be loyal and supportive in return.

The Casa di Fortuna sat on top of a hill, a square, solid stone structure surrounded by garden. It had once been the estate manager's home but the current manager had built his own house and Sofia had decided to make the old house her new marital home. A variety of pickup trucks and vans sat in the driveway announcing the presence of builders and tradesmen.

Dante vaulted out of the car, Topsy falling in step behind him, gazing up at the sheer height and width of him, shaken afresh by the total size of him and the utter impossibility of ignoring him. They had barely walked into the hall when Gaetano Massaro, whose building company was in charge of renovating the house, descended the stairs to greet them. 'Topsy...' He inclined his curly dark head and grinned in his usual friendly fashion before addressing Dante and offering to show him round.

Of course the two men knew each other, not least because Gaetano was also involved in the fund-raising for the local child's leukaemia treatment. In the airy kitchen Topsy dug her phone from her bag so that she could take photos to show Sofia. The tiles had been redone in a different shade and design at Sofia's request. Her employer was very particular about details and Topsy fully understood why. Not only married but also a mother at the tender age of seven-

teen, Sofia had moved into her husband's ances-
tral castle and had not been allowed to change
anything to suit her own taste. By all accounts,
Dante's father had been something of a domestic tyrant and a control freak. The Casa di Fortuna, therefore, was very much the contessa's
first real home.

The decorator joined Topsy and took her into
the cloakroom to inspect the illuminated mirror that had been installed. Playing safe, Topsy
took a photo of it as well and then lingered in
the doorway, watching Dante and Gaetano chat.
Beside Dante, Gaetano looked small, slight and
boyish and yet it was only three days since she
had decided that Gaetano was attractive enough
to date and she had agreed to have dinner with
him in his family's restaurant that very evening.
Gaetano was good company, she reminded herself impatiently, which was all she required in
a man. He didn't need to send her temperature
rocketing as well.

Dante crossed the hall. 'Show me the downstairs reception area,' he instructed, dismiss-

ing Gaetano with an almost invisible nod of his handsome dark head.

Behind Dante's back, the builder rolled his eyes in mock amusement at the manner in which Dante had virtually ignored his offer to be his guide and Topsy coloured, narrow shoulders lifting back as if she was bracing herself while she led the way into the very large open-plan area that several rooms had been sacrificed to create. Floor-to-ceiling glass doors led out onto a terrace at the back of the house.

'It's much more contemporary than I was expecting,' Dante admitted lazily, his deep accented voice fingering a trail of awareness down her taut spine. 'For some reason I thought the two of them would recreate the Eighties here.'

'I think your mother's tired of living with the past and looking to the future for inspiration.' Topsy pressed a wall button and the glass doors whirred smoothly back. 'All this took an enormous amount of planning.'

'How much input did Vittore have?' Dante asked.

'Very little…' Strolling outside into the shade cast by the roof above, Topsy laughed softly. 'He doesn't have much interest in house interiors but I think he was also aware from the outset that this was very much your mother's dream and he didn't want to spoil it for her by imposing his views.'

'You appear to have a high opinion of Vittore,' he commented with a derogatory edge to his tone that suggested he didn't share her outlook.

'I speak as I find. I've yet to see or hear him do anything to detract from that opinion,' Topsy responded easily, trying not to resent his judgemental attitude towards the older man, telling herself that was none of her business and refusing to let Dante make her feel uncomfortable.

And yet he managed that feat without even trying, she acknowledged in dismay as she looked up at him, striving to be fearless and frank rather than nervous and wary of her every word. His stunning green eyes glittered with high-voltage energy in the sunlight in which he stood, for he was much more at home in the heat of midday than she was. He looked hostile and intimidating and she was in the act of stepping back from him when his hands came out and closed round her slender forearms, halting her into a startled retreat.

The instant he made physical contact, another kind of energy hummed into being inside Topsy, taking her body out of control and into a dangerous state of extreme awareness. For a split second she couldn't breathe. Her breasts swelled beneath her clothing, the tender tips straining into tight buds while a sensation of heat pulsed almost unbearably at her feminine core. 'What are you doing?' she said breathlessly, struggling to pull air into her depleted lungs as his hands trailed down her arms to close round her wrists instead.

'What I wanted to do the minute I first saw you,' he husked, pressing her back into the cooling shade of the wall. 'Discover how you taste.'

'No, thanks,' Topsy told him thinly, fighting her weakness with all her might even though she was insanely tempted to move forward and sink into the hard muscular heat of him and find out what that mutual tasting would feel like.

A derisive smile that unnerved her slashed his hard, handsome mouth. 'The way you look at me, do you seriously expect me to believe that?'

Shock that he could study her in such a way and yet show his scorn filled her and momentarily she hesitated, struggling to compute that strange combination of desire and contempt. That tiny instant of hesitation, however, was fatal. His mouth swooped down on hers with a hard, hungry urgency that shot every sensible thought right out of her head as though it had never existed. She *felt* as she had never *felt* before, burning waves of reaction slivering through her entire body, whipped up to a storm with every carnal plunge of his tongue. Heat burst low in her pelvis, tightening her nipples to the point of pain and shooting raw stabs of need to the very heart of her. Inflamed by her own response, she strained back against him, just as he bent even more with a growl of frustration to curve his hands below her hips to lift her and pin her in place between his body and the wall behind her. She felt entrapped, excited, *wild* for more…

His hands roved across her back, came up to curve to the sides of her face while her fingers delved happily into his luxuriant black hair, delighting in the springy depths. The scent of him flared her nostrils, clean, hot male laced with an elusive spicy scent of soap or cologne. She breathed him in headily like an addict.

'You're way too small to do this standing up,' Dante complained against her swollen, reddened mouth.

That remark cut through the haze of desire that had engulfed her, innate apprehension gripping her. Do *what*? Suddenly she was aware again, conscious that her legs were pinned round him and that her skirt had to be somewhere up round her waist. Shock reverberated through her like a hard wakening slap on the face. 'Put me down!' she exclaimed in horror. 'We shouldn't be doing this!'

Dante lowered her slowly, reluctantly, back

down to the tiles while with frantic hands she yanked down her skirt to cover her exposed thighs. She was appalled by her own loss of control and the false message of availability she had no doubt given him by responding to him in such a way. She didn't play around and she didn't tease men either, and as her stomach brushed against his hard, taut length on the passage back to standing on her own feet again she knew he was in no mood to be teased. He was aroused, fully aroused, and a wave of discomfited pink engulfed her heart-shaped face. Her brain told her it had only been a kiss, but no kiss, no man's touch had ever had that explosive an effect on Topsy before, and even as she stole a glance up at him she knew she wanted to drag him back into her arms and have him do it again. Hands unsteady, she reached for the shoulder bag that had fallen on the patio and anchored it round her shoulder again.

'Is that a "no" in Topsy land or simply a prudent "not here, not now"?' Dante enquired with terrifyingly smooth assurance.

'It's a no, never. I'm sorry. That shouldn't have happened. I work for your mother. I don't think she would like me—'

'I assure you that it is many, many years since my mother worried about who I take to my bed,' Dante sliced in very drily.

Flustered and intensely ill at ease, Topsy walked away from him on stiff legs to the edge of the patio, perspiration beading her upper lip as the hot sun beat down on her. Drowning in mortification and consternation at the passion that had exploded between them, Topsy breathed in jerkily. 'But in the circumstances it's not a good idea, let's face it,' she reasoned steadily. 'I've no intention of going to bed with you anyway so there's no point starting something that won't go to the finish that you expect.'

'I'll take you into Florence this evening…we'll dine out,' Dante declared as though she hadn't spoken.

Topsy froze, registering that she had made a mistake that would bring punishment home to her fast. 'I've already got a date tonight.'

Ashamed as she was of her behaviour, Topsy could not resist looking at him again and the astonishment that briefly flashed across his handsome features in reaction to that admission only increased her embarrassment.

'I don't share—cancel him,' Dante advised, taken aback by her statement while wondering if she was reluctant to dally with him because she already had Vittore in her sights. Certainly she could not hope to keep two men in the same household interested.

'No, I won't do that, not when this was a mistake…but for your information, it's a first date. I haven't cheated on anyone,' she confided on a driven note of pride. 'I wouldn't do that.'

Dante shrugged a broad shoulder as if such restraints had no meaning for him and she was even less impressed by that attitude. 'We're both single. I want you and you want me—'

'For a moment of madness,' Topsy quipped. 'But I'm glad it didn't go any further.'

'Liar…' Dante murmured soft and low.

That fast she wanted to slap him so hard that

her palm tingled and she flashed him a flaring look of such seething anger that he looked taken aback. But if Topsy was furious with him, she was equally furious with herself. She had come to Italy with a real purpose and, while she had certainly planned to enjoy the freedom of meeting men without family supervision, a fleeting affair with her employer's son would be as inappropriate as it was humiliating. Her stubborn chin came up just as Gaetano strolled out to join them, flicking her a curious glance as if he had picked up on the tension in the air.

'Anything I can help you with?' he prompted Dante. 'Do you want to see the upper floor?'

'Another time,' Dante deferred with no expression at all. He had known the Massaro family all his life and he was well aware that Gaetano would be out of his depth and drowning with a little schemer like Topsy. Was Gaetano being used as cover for the girl's interest in Vittore? If his marriage crashed and burned, Vittore would be a wealthy divorcee well worth pursuing. But if money was Topsy's goal, and what else could it be, why was she turning down Dante, who was a much more lucrative target? His face set into forbidding lines. Of course Vittore would be easier meat, he reasoned, and some women preferred older men. That suspicion still rankled with a male who had not, in living memory, been turned down by a woman.

Topsy settled back into the Pagani sports car and strove to rigorously ignore the thunderous undertones in the atmosphere. She had said no and he wasn't pleased that she had but she had made the right decision; she *knew* she had. Getting involved with Dante would be disastrous even though she wasn't foolish enough to imagine that he was considering anything more than a brief sexually entertaining fling. Although she had no doubt that he would be seriously disappointed by her lack of bedroom expertise. She knew that rich international bankers didn't seriously date humble employees unless said humble employee was possessed of extraordinary beauty. The only exception to the rule was her sister Emmie, who had ended up marrying her Greek billionaire boss, Bastian Christou.

While Saffy, Zahir's adored queen, and her twin Emmie could stop traffic with their looks, Topsy had long since resigned herself to being the plain one of the family, having inherited neither the height, the flawless features nor the blonde manes bestowed by their mother's genes. Kat was a redhead and stunning as well. At an early age, Topsy had grasped that her own most notable talent was her powerful intellect but that being cleverer than most of the people around her was not so much a gift as a curse. It certainly didn't make you popular, she reflected, thinking of the brutal bullying she had endured at primary school. Being different from the norm could entail paying a high price.

Her mobile phone rang in her bag and she dug it out to answer it.

'It's Mikhail. I'm in Milan and you're not where you're supposed to be,' her brother-in-law told her succinctly, making her lose colour and freeze in dismay at her end of the phone, quite unprepared to deal with the bombshell that her cover story had blown up in her face when she least expected it.

'I had no idea you were coming to Italy,' she muttered, nervous tension gripping her for Mikhail, Kat's husband, was not a man she felt she could lie to with impunity.

'And unfortunately for you your school friend, Gabrielle, decided to confess and admitted that you were actually staying in Tuscany. We'll meet in Florence tomorrow for lunch and you'll explain then *fully* what's going on,' he decreed without an ounce of hesitation, making her feel like one of his many minions who leapt to do his bidding and fulfil his every request.

'I'm afraid that won't be possible,' Topsy said stiffly.

'*Make* it possible,' her Russian brother-in-law advised in a grim tone that brooked no argument. 'I'll send a limo to pick you up at noon.'

'That won't be necessary. I'll meet you if you tell me where to go.'

'I decide what's necessary and don't feed your

sisters any more nonsense or tell my wife anything that might worry her,' he told her sternly.

Topsy swallowed her growing ire with difficulty, feeling like a dog being yanked by a choke
chain, both powerless and bullied. 'I wouldn't
risk doing that.'

'Wouldn't you? It would undoubtedly distress
Kat to learn that you felt the need to lie to her,'
Mikhail breathed harshly and cut the connec-
tion without another word.

Topsy breathed in deep and slow and thrust
her phone back in her bag. Mikhail was furious
with her, for naturally he would only see the situation from his wife's point of view and he was
fanatically protective when it came to her sister.
Even so, it didn't matter what he intended to say
to her in Florence, she wasn't quitting Tuscany
and returning to London on his say-so.

On that rebellious thought she lifted her chin,
her innate obstinacy kicking in. Somehow, some
way her family had to come to terms with the
reality that she was an adult with a right to freedom and independence and if that meant that she

made mistakes, so be it! Her sisters had had the chance to grow up and explore the world without interference. Why shouldn't she claim the same right?

'You seem upset...trouble?' Dante prompted softly.

'No...er...not exactly,' she responded tightly.

'Your family?' Dante queried, shooting the Pagani off the road and into a farm track without even thinking about the sharp curiosity driving him to interrupt their journey.

Not even having noticed that the car had parked, Topsy stiffened even more defensively, reminding herself that she owed no one any explanations that she did not wish to make. 'Er... no, an old flame,' she fibbed, determined to retain her anonymity and persuade her fabulously wealthy relations to stay on the sidelines for once.

But a sensation like ice was already trickling down her spine because if Mikhail Kusnirovich knew where she was, she was convinced he would also have demanded an investigative report on her current living arrangements. Would he guess about Vittore? Would he realise exactly what his sister-in-law was doing at the Castello Leonetti? Could *nothing* in her life be considered private? Lunch had been arranged and Mikhail never entered any meeting unprepared. Suddenly ferocious resentment was bubbling up through her tiny body. She had believed she had temporarily escaped her family's suffocating hold but their reach was longer than she had appreciated. It was typical that she had not been warned that her brother-in-law was coming to Italy and planning to visit her.

'Are you scared of this man?' Dante pressed, level black brows drawing together in a frown as he leant closer.

'Of course I'm not scared!' Topsy forced a laugh because she was undeniably afraid of the emotional blackmail her family utilised to make her toe the line, the subtle guilt-inducing reminders that she owed her happy childhood and everything she had become to their love, support and loyalty. She, alone of her sisters and owing only to her young age at the time, had escaped her mother's neglectful care without sustaining any permanent damage and if her siblings were quite unable to accept that she no longer required their guiding hand, was that their fault? Or was it *hers*? Maybe it was some obvious lack in her that had convinced them she still needed to have her every move policed, she reflected worriedly.

Dante's shrewd green eyes were pinned to the fluctuating emotions on Topsy's intensely expressive little face. As someone who didn't *do* emotion, he was fascinated, never having seen anyone betray so many changes of emotion and all within the space of seconds. Dark glossy strands of silken hair fanned her cheek, the exact match of the long flickering lashes framing her anxious amber eyes above the flushed rise of her delicate cheekbones. No, she was not a raving beauty but there was a softness about her, a seeming honesty and vulnerability that had the strangest appeal to a male accustomed to more sophisticated and controlled women. He blinked, disconcerted by that uncharacteristic thought. And that fast desire kicked in hard, tensing every lean muscle in his powerful length with an almost exquisite surge of arousal.

'You may not be scared but you *are* upset,' he contradicted, fighting to stay focused on the conversation but his mind in another place entirely as he imagined igniting all that obvious pent-up passion for his own benefit and riding her raw in his bed to sate the painfully strong hunger punching through him.

'No, I'm not…it was just a stupid phone call… and sometimes I overreact.' Topsy was mesmerised by the force of his stunning green eyes holding hers and she could hardly breathe for the excitement gripping her while she scanned the handsome features above hers. In terms of the physical, he really was the most absolutely beautiful man. A supersonic quiet had fallen inside the car so that she could hear her own breathing, air sawing in and out of her throat as if she had been running a marathon, her heart racing like an express train behind breasts that were swollen and tender tipped, that same terrifying heat rising between her legs.

Dante lifted an elegant hand and slowly and with great dexterity and deceptive calm wound long fingers into the glossy mane of her hair to hold her in place. He was in a car and in broad daylight at a place where anyone might see and recognise him. He didn't know what he was doing but would never ever have admitted that a much more primal drive than intelligence had suppressed his innate caution and freed him from inhibition. The seething hunger was clawing at him like an angry beast, the pulse at his swollen groin threatening to control him as he brought her to him and kissed her with scorching heat, his tongue delving deep, his body firing as she loosed a strangled whimper of response than only made him harder.

Dante reached for her and lifted her out of the seat to bring her down over his spread thighs. He had never wanted anything so much as he wanted the hot, tight, wet heat of her body at that moment and the shockingly new strength of that wanting overpowering everything else inflamed him.

'What are you doing?' Topsy gasped, having got feverishly lost in that passionate kiss. He touched her and every sensible thought, every shred of self-discipline vanished as though it had never been. She studied that perfectly moulded, wide, sensual mouth, which felt so firm and sexy and unbelievably good on hers, and trembled, needing more, every skin cell evidently pro-grammed to want more.

Slumberous green eyes below black lashes sur-veyed her. 'I think you know the answer to that, *cara mia.*'

His fingers glided up the sensitive inside of her thighs and her heart rate went from fast to racing in seconds. Tell him no, a voice urged in the back of her head, but the craving for him to go further was too strong for her to fight. In conflict with herself, she shivered, breasts with beaded tips pushing against a bra that seemed too tight to contain her, inner muscles she hadn't known she had clenching tight at the very thought of greater intimacy. She tensed as a fingertip eased beneath the lace edge of her panties and she knew she should move, knew she should be telling him, *no*, she wasn't this kind of a woman. But just then, with Dante Leonetti's hand on her all too responsive flesh, she knew she was exactly that kind of woman and she was quite unable to resist the temptation he offered. She trembled, gazed down into glittering emerald eyes as bright as gemstones and he found the place he sought, circled, teased, brushed, stroked while she moaned and tried not to lose herself in the terrible maddening pleasure of his caresses. But her body was on another plane of existence entirely, quivering and burning and leaping with new sensation.

'D-Dante…' she pronounced shakily at her second attempt to find her voice.

'*Sì*…' he purred like a jungle cat, yanking her head down to claim her already reddened mouth with fierce and passionate urgency. 'Let Gaetano down gently—he's a nice boy. I want you naked and hungry in my bed and tonight I will satisfy your every fantasy. Now come for me...'

And with a skilled flick of his hand, the quaking intensity became more than she could withstand and this great whoosh of sensational excitement engulfed her straining body, jolting her with wave after wave of almost unbearable pleasure. She heard herself cry out in ecstasy.

Even though his body was rigid with arousal and self-control, Dante was surprisingly satisfied as he rested his tousled dark head back against the head rest. He readjusted her panties, smoothed down her skirt where she knelt on his lap. He had put his mark on her: she was *his* now and he had no objection to admitting that she was the most exciting woman he had had in his arms in a very long time. He could not believe that she could be engaged in some sleazy relationship with Vittore at the same time as she was responding to him and, *Dio mio*, that was some response, he savoured sensually.

Shock and embarrassment roared through her in a head-spinning whirl and she scrambled off him in sudden horror, her face red as fire, her eyes momentarily closing in an agony of mortification. What had she done? *What had she done?* As she moved she saw another car parked a few yards away. 'Oh, good grief, there's another car nearby…we've been *seen*!' she gasped, stricken.

Dante didn't bat a single magnificent eyelash. 'My bodyguards, you don't need to worry about them.'

'Bodyguards?' she yelped in even greater dismay, because she knew all about bodyguards, teams of men who operated in all her sisters' lives as protection and supervision.

'I go nowhere without them. The bank insists,' Dante said, unconcerned.

Biting her lip, Topsy did up her seat belt. You *slut*, she told herself, her body still humming with treacherous pleasure and frank astonishment at what he had made her feel. Even so, his erotic approach had made her feel ridiculously virginal and ignorant, so far out of her depth and foolish she could not even bring herself to look at him again. She would certainly never ever look in the direction of his wretched bodyguards, knowing very well that bodyguards were just as human as everybody else and equally prone to gossip. Had that not been why Mikhail moved her bodyguard Vlad to other duties when he considered that they had become too 'friendly'. Prior to that, she had heard some very amusing tales from Vlad about his experiences, his Russian reserve crumpling around her. Mikhail had teased her about being a femme fatale for mortifying months afterwards yet nothing had ever happened between her and Vlad. If only she could say the same thing of Dante Leonetti!

CHAPTER THREE

DANTE WATCHED TOPSY bounce out of the castle and down the steps to greet Gaetano in his Porsche. She looked incredibly young and pretty in a fuchsia-pink dress and ridiculously high heels. He snatched in a breath, teeth clenching as she flashed her shapely legs climbing in. It was ridiculous: she *should* have cancelled the date. The very idea of Gaetano getting close enough to touch her made Dante incredibly tense. Yet he was not a possessive man and had often enjoyed non-exclusive relationships that enabled him to retain his freedom. Possibly it was because he hadn't bedded her yet, he ruminated with brooding intensity.

'Is that Gaetano picking up Topsy?' his mother enquired from where she was still seated with Vittore at the dining table behind her son.

'I hope he behaves himself—not like that Siccardi boy.'

'Siccardi? Bruno Siccardi?' Dante referred to one of their neighbours, a young and handsome playboy known for his wildness. 'She went out with him as well? *Maledizione*, she does get around!'

'And why shouldn't she?' Sofia enquired. 'She's cooped up all day every day with us and we're middle-aged and not a lot of fun.'

'Speak for yourself,' Vittore teased. 'I think I'm just as much fun as the Siccardi boy!'

'What happened to him?' Dante prompted.

'Oh, she had to fight him off, said he had more hands than an octopus and that was the end of him,' his mother supplied cheerfully. 'Topsy's no pushover.'

But she hadn't fought *him* off, Dante reflected with positive relish, using that recollection to suppress his exasperation with her at her determination to keep that date. It was a novelty to be with a woman who wasn't falling over herself to meet his every demand and expectation but that didn't mean he liked it and he was confident that her attitude would soon change.

Topsy was embarrassingly conscious of Gaetano's family's very hopeful and constant scrutiny of their table. So far, she had met his mamma, his papa, one sister and two younger brothers, for the restaurant in the village was a family affair and every one of his relatives was delighted to see Gaetano dining out in female company. Gaetano had already taken her step by painful step through the story of how his childhood sweetheart and former fiancée, Daria, had gone off to study for a further degree and had fallen madly in love with another man and dumped him, leaving him with a half-built marital dream home.

'Your liveliness reminded me of her…a little,' Gaetano had told her, clearly thinking that was a compliment until she advised him that the best thing possible for him would be to seek a woman who reminded him not at all of his lost love. By that stage both of them knew that they would never be anything to each other than friends and Topsy didn't have to feel the slightest bit guilty at not having experienced any romantic spark in his direction.

'Dante seemed…er…attentive,' Gaetano selected, eyes dancing with amusement. 'When he brought you to the house.'

Topsy blushed furiously. 'I don't think we'd have much in common.'

Gaetano nodded thoughtfully. 'You're thinking of his wealth and his fancy title but it would be a mistake to assume that Dante always had it easy.'

Topsy didn't correct his assumption. 'Hasn't he?' she pressed, full of a curiosity she could not suppress.

Gaetano grimaced. 'When he was sixteen, my father found him lying by the side of the road one night. He'd been badly beaten up, broken nose, broken ribs, in fact every finger of one hand was broken. He wouldn't tell my father or the police who had done it.' Gaetano hesitated.

'My parents always believed it was his father, Aldo. The old count had a filthy temper.'

Topsy had paled in shock, mentally picturing one of Dante's long-fingered elegant hands, and she swallowed hard on her nausea. 'If that's true, he must have had a tough time as a child.'

That conversation was still lingering on her mind when she was climbing the stairs at the castle at the end of their evening. Just goes to show, never judge by appearances, she conceded ruefully just as she rounded the corner of the landing and entered the corridor to find herself face-to-face with the very man occupying her brain to the exclusion of all else.

'Dante!' she exclaimed, startled by his unexpected appearance.

Dante scanned her face with intent gleaming eyes of green. 'Your lipstick isn't even smudged,' he commented with unconcealed satisfaction.

'And what the heck is that supposed to mean?' Topsy flung back at him, dark hair dancing round her slight shoulders as she tossed her head in annoyance.

'You didn't let him touch you.'

Topsy sucked in a deep, angry breath that filled her lungs to capacity. 'And that is your business *because*...?'

'Tonight you're mine,' Dante informed her with a level of unmistakable assurance that drove her breath right back out of her lungs again, deflating her when she could least afford the weakness.

A split second later, Dante did nothing to help her condition because he did something even more shocking: bending down, scooping her off her feet as though she were a doll and anchoring both arms tightly round her.

'Have you gone insane? What are you doing?' Topsy exclaimed, keeping her voice low though because she did not want anyone to come investigating, indeed would have done just about anything to avoid being caught in such a compromising position by anyone living at the castle.

'Stop acting dim—you know exactly what I'm

doing!' Dante asserted, boldly thrusting wide a door and striding into a room she had never entered before for the simple reason that it was *his* bedroom.

'What on earth do you think you're playing at?' Topsy yelped as he put her down on the giant four-poster bed with scant ceremony.

'You went on your date to which I very generously did not object.'

'You've got no blasted right to object!' Topsy hissed back at him full volume. 'No right at all!'

His features set rigid, his spectacular bone structure prominent. 'I want you to spend the night with me.'

'And even if you'd asked like any normal man, the answer would *still* be no!' Topsy slung at him furiously, flushed and all of a quiver from the assumption he appeared to have made about her and anything but grateful to be forced to relive those deeply embarrassing and heated minutes in his car, which had led to his misapprehension that she would be so easily available that she would simply fall into his bed the instant he expressed the desire.

Dante dealt her an incredulous look from scorching green eyes. *'No?'* he repeated, as though it was a word he had never heard before from a woman in the bedroom.

Topsy scrambled off his bed, retrieved a shoe that had dropped off and wedged her foot back into it at the same time as she smoothed down her rucked skirt. 'I'm sorry if I gave you the wrong impression this afternoon but I'm not going to sleep with you,' she told him squarely.

She reminded Dante of a determined little bird rearranging her bright-feathered plumage, her slightly snub nose in the air, her heart-shaped face pink as one of his mother's precious roses. 'Yet you want me,' he breathed between clenched teeth, for *all* he had thought about all evening when he should have been catching up on work was his fantasy of getting her in his bed where she belonged.

'This afternoon…er…well that was an aberration and entirely your own fault,' Topsy told him roundly, furious at the situation he had put her in, fighting her mortification that he could have thought she would be that easy. Of course when she hadn't objected to that shameless little session of intimacy in the car, could she really blame him? And it did not help that when she looked at that gorgeous dark angel face of his she felt breathless and boneless and prone to reliving every madly exciting moment of his touch.

'How was it *my* fault?' Dante demanded.

'You shouldn't be so good at seduction,' Topsy responded with every evidence of conviction in that belief. 'If I'd had a moment to stop and consider, it would never have happened and we wouldn't be having this conversation now.'

Dante was furious with her for the ambiguous signals she had fed him, but for a split second he was startled to realise he was also on the edge of bursting out laughing at that response. 'Perhaps we should begin again,' he breathed instead, his hard mouth curling a little, for he had never said that to a woman in his life before, but then he could also not recall ever being quite so hot to have one.

'No, we're not going to begin anything!' Topsy exclaimed, and then bent down as her heel dug into a sheet of paper on the rug, detaching it with careful fingers and lifting it up to see the columns of figures. 'Oh, that's wrong...'

Already detaching from her hand the sheet that had escaped from the file that had fallen to the floor when he put her on his bed, Dante frowned down at her. 'What's wrong?'

Topsy peered over his arm and stabbed a finger at one column. 'It's added up wrong.'

'Of course it isn't,' he responded impatiently, setting the document down on the file beside his laptop.

'Dante, I have a doctorate in advanced maths and the one thing I do know is figures and I assure you that that final entry is a mistake,' Topsy said drily.

'A doctorate in advanced maths?' Dante echoed, studying her with incredulous eyes while wondering what someone with such a background was doing working for his mother.

Topsy nodded, wishing she had kept her mouth shut while carefully edging back towards the door.

Dante stalked her like a fox set on cornering a hen. 'I don't want you to leave. I want you to explain why we can't start again.'

Topsy groaned out loud. She hated these conversations with men, for in her experience they almost always went the same way and the men got disgruntled, unable to understand why she wouldn't just drop into bed with them to scratch a sexual itch. 'Look, all you want is sex and that's not enough for me.'

Dante dealt her a pained appraisal, by which time she was plastered up against the back of his bedroom door, one hand curled round the door knob. 'Doesn't everybody want sex?'

'I'm not looking for love and marriage either but there has to be something more,' Topsy contended, because she had considered the subject in depth and had drawn up a list of desirable male attributes, none of which he met.

An eloquent black brow rose. 'Something... *more*?'

'I'm not into casual sex,' she pointed out, almost adding *any* kind of sex but holding that revealing admission back. 'You don't know me or even care about me and we're not similar or even complementary in character,' she pointed out very seriously. 'I mean, when did you last wear a pair of jeans?'

Not since his student days. Dante was feeling increasingly like a male version of *Alice in Wonderland* who had fallen down the rabbit hole only to emerge into an incomprehensible world. 'Jeans?' he repeated thunderously at what he saw as yet another red herring. Similar or complementary in character? What planet was she from?

'You toured a building site today in an Armani suit and gold cuff links. I don't dress up as a rule, don't like that appearances sort of thing that people get hung up about. What on earth would we talk about or do together?'

Dante was much more interested in the doing than the talking and he leant forward, bracing his hands on either side of her face. 'I don't think entertainment would cause us much of a problem,' he husked in a low-pitched growl that raised colour in her cheeks again, the clean, spicy, male scent of him entrapping her like a covert spell. 'Mentioning stuff like clothing is just so superficial—I'm surprised at you.'

'But superficial, ruthless and mercenary is what you are!' Topsy protested helplessly, feeling crowded at the few inches that were now all that separated their bodies.

'We would have maths in common,' Dante countered with something that felt dangerously akin to desperation. 'I'm terrific at maths.'

'Oh…' Topsy was also thinking about his reputation as a philanthropist, striving to cram him under an acceptable label on her all-important list of ideal male traits. But there was just no way he would fit there. He wasn't modest or soothing and she seriously doubted that he could cook or clean. All he had going for him was sex appeal and a very immodest amount of it, she reasoned feverishly.

Dante skated a fingertip along the sultry line of her luscious mouth. 'Let me make love to you.'

'Don't use words you don't mean. It wouldn't be making love, it would be grubby sex!' Topsy snapped bluntly. 'And I'm worth more than that!'

Dante frowned, green eyes radiating resolve while his face took on a sardonic edge at her use of that insulting label, 'grubby'. 'How much more?'

'You really don't give up easily, do you?' Topsy framed, her mouth still tingling from his touch, but his bold determination was starting to intimidate her because he was like a guided missile locked onto target. 'It's just we really would be wasting each other's time.'

'I don't *do* grubby, *cara mia*,' Dante whispered. 'I *want* you to waste my time.'

'My goodness, I'm so tired I can hardly stay

awake!' Topsy lied in dismay, carefully screening her mouth as though she were yawning in a last-ditch effort to conclude the confrontation.

'Tired?' Dante repeated, unimpressed, but he retreated a disconcerted step.

Mercifully he had moved just enough to unblock the door and Topsy flipped round and opened it fast. 'Night, Dante!' she called over her shoulder and sped off fast.

Dante swore and not under his breath. She was a tease, nothing but a tease, he reckoned furiously. Maybe it was an act, designed to lure him in deeper and increase his desire for her. He could not remember when a woman had last knocked him into pursuit mode. In fact he could not recall *ever* having to pursue or persuade a woman. He needed a cold shower. He flicked a glance at the empty bed and cursed again. Jeans…similar or complementary characters? *Superficial, ruthless, mercenary?* Self-evidently, she was a nutcase. Furthermore, ruthless was a compliment, not a personality trait worthy of censure. He had had a narrow escape, he told himself impatiently, and if she was playing some childish girlie game with him, she would soon discover that she was indeed wasting her time for he wasn't that desperate. She exasperated him. He headed for the cold shower with anger in his glittering eyes. There was a world of women out there, beautiful, sophisticated women, who didn't talk rubbish, insult him or lead him on only to change their minds at the last possible moment.

Having climbed into her comfortable bed, Topsy checked the list in the back of her diary that she had written when she was eighteen and trying to make sense of the almost incomprehensible dating scene at university. She had never fit in, never met her soul mate but had truly believed that he was out there somewhere. Dante met only one of her listed requirements: he was clever. But clever wasn't quite the right word, she reflected ruefully: conniving and unscrupulous came closer to how she would have described him. And she had no regrets, she told herself urgently. She was much too sensible to surrender her virginity to a male who only awakened her hormones and didn't give a damn about her.

A little voice in the recesses of her less scrupulous conscience pointed out speciously that Dante was very probably very good in bed and would almost certainly make a great first lover. After all, it wasn't as if *she* were looking for love or commitment, so perhaps it was a little unjust to blame him for a flaw she suffered from herself. Some day she would fall in love and want commitment, but she imagined that day was very far away and she fiercely suppressed that dangerous little voice in her brain.

Tomorrow, she would be lunching with Mikhail, who was as devious and manipulative as any Machiavelli when it came to delivering what would please her sister Kat most. Topsy knew she would have to keep her wits about her and make sure that she stood her ground.

CHAPTER FOUR

THE FOLLOWING MORNING, Dante used the back stairs to return to his bedroom after a heavy workout session in the basement gym. On edge after a restive night, a freezing-cold shower and the conviction that he had been manipulated by some means he had yet to identify, he was not in a good mood. Almost more infuriatingly when he had finally risen early to concentrate on work instead, he had discovered that she had been correct about that figure being wrong in the file. Yet she had only glanced at the page! How could she possibly have recognised a mistake that fast? He was about to stride through a doorway when he heard Topsy's distinctive voice and Vittore's, both of them talking in low voices somewhere out of his view.

'I can't make it today,' Topsy was telling the

older man. 'I should have told you last night but I couldn't mention it in front of Sofia.'

'Of course not. We'll have to go to Florence some other day.' Dante's stepfather sighed. 'As long as Sofia doesn't realise what we're up to, we have nothing to worry about.'

'Would she be annoyed?' Topsy prompted.

'Are you joking?' Vittore groaned. 'After the last time, she said she'd kill me! I have to get it right this time.'

While Dante hovered with a frown, the voices died away as the couple retreated. What the hell was all that about? His original notion that Topsy might be involved with his stepfather had dwindled, but after that cosy exchange suspicion ran rampant through him again. Why were Vittore and his wife's secretary whispering in corners? Why were they meeting up in Florence in secret? How could that be innocent? What had to be hidden from his mother? *After the last time, she'd kill me!* A previous act of infidelity, Dante decided in disgust. Was that what Vittore had been referring to?

He did not like to think that his mother would even consider forgiving and forgetting such a betrayal, but he could not overlook the fact that she had spent many years married to a man who had *forced* her to close her eyes to his infidelity and accept it. His parent could be slipping back into that unfortunate pattern, refusing to see the truth that this time around she had no reason to feel that she had no choice but to accept such behaviour.

It was ten minutes to midday and Topsy was dressed for lunch in Florence, her curvy figure simply clad in a green sundress with shoestring straps. Tense though she was, Vittore had contrived to put a smile on her face. That cliché about try, try, try again when you got it wrong might have been specially coined for Sofia's husband. Vittore wanted to give his wife a piece of jewellery that she would actually like and wear and, since Vittore had a natural love of bling and sparkle while Sofia preferred plain and elegant, her bridegroom had repeatedly got his gift

choices wrong. That was why Topsy was to accompany Vittore to the design studio to choose
a piece that her employer might genuinely appreciate for her birthday.

Topsy joined Sofia to briefly discuss the floral
arrangements for the fancy-dress ball and then
headed downstairs, stiffening as the ancient bell
over the massive gothic front door rang noisily
and checking her watch: it was five to twelve.
When she saw the hulking bodyguard on the
step, she recognised him as Danilo, the head of
Mikhail's security, and, while she wondered if
the forbidding older man had been sent to collect her in an effort to daunt her, her soft mouth
firmed.

'Where's your luggage?' Danilo enquired with
a frown.

Topsy's heart sank. Had she misunderstood
Mikhail? Was he expecting her to simply pack
up and go home with him to London? Her chin
came up. 'I'm coming back here after lunch. I'm
not leaving.'

Danilo made no comment, which didn't surprise her because he was not a chatty man. He stood out on the step instead wielding his mobile phone and talking in Russian, undoubtedly checking up on his employer's expectations.

As she lifted her handbag from the hall chair where she had left it earlier she saw Dante poised in the doorway of his study, lean, strong, dark face taut. At the sight of him, her heart jumped as though someone had closed a hand round the organ and squeezed. His straight dark brows were low over dazzling green eyes thickly enhanced by lashes black as coal as he gazed back at her. He was *so* beautiful. Without warning she was reliving the touch of his finger on her lips the night before, the little bristles of dangerous pleasure that had travelled down her spine to warm secret places, making her breasts ache and her knees tremble. Colour washed her cheeks, a hunger she couldn't deny stirring like a threatening storm.

'Are you ready to leave?' Danilo prompted impatiently.

Topsy spun back to the older man and walked

out of the door. Unfortunately the heat of the summer sun did nothing to cool her overheated skin.

The limo had barely driven off when Dante crossed the wide hall, inclining his arrogant dark head in acknowledgement of the younger man waiting by the car that had just drawn up outside. He had decided to have Topsy followed. He wanted to know who she was meeting in Florence and why she had been shaken by the invitation. The more he learned about her, the closer he might come to working out what was going on at the castle. Everybody around him was acting weird, he thought impatiently. His mother was lying about on a chaise longue like some fragile Victorian lady suffering from a decline, while Vittore was whistling under his breath and whispering in dark corners with the hired help.

Topsy's brother-in-law looked grim when he greeted her at the door of his hotel suite. A waiter was already setting out food from a heated trolley and hovering. With a flick of an imperious hand, Mikhail dismissed him and urged Topsy to sit down.

'So, what's going on? What are you up to?' he asked Topsy baldly before she even got her bottom onto a seat.

'That's my business,' Topsy replied quietly as she tucked into her starter.

'If it threatens Kat's peace of mind, it's mine,' Mikhail overruled without hesitation. 'She's pregnant again, by the way.'

That announcement took Topsy by surprise because her sister suffered from fertility problems and having had IVF to conceive her twins had tried it again but, sadly, without success. 'Oh, my goodness, that's wonderful news!' she exclaimed, knowing how much her eldest sister had longed for another child. 'But…er…how?'

'It happened naturally this time but you can understand why I won't have her upset at the moment,' he pointed out levelly. 'It's cards-on-the-table time, Topsy. If the draw at the castle is Dante Leonetti, you need to be aware of the kind of lifestyle he leads.'

'Dante is not the draw and, yes, I do have a secret but it's private and nothing to do with anyone else in the family, nor would it matter to them,' Topsy proffered with conviction. 'I'm almost twenty-four years old, Mikhail. Don't expect me to explain everything I do.'

Her brother-in-law compressed his hard mouth. 'I still remember you in your school uniform.'

'And how many years ago is that?' Topsy sighed. 'I'm a big girl now.'

'No, you're physically tiny and still very naïve,' Mikhail countered impatiently. 'But don't lay that at my door. Your sisters refuse to accept that baby has grown up.'

At that unexpected admission, which implied some understanding of her plight, Topsy relaxed a tiny bit. 'I know. It's ridiculous to get to my age and have to lie to lead my own life.'

Mikhail sat back into his chair. 'Dante Leonetti?' he queried with a raised brow. 'How is he involved in this?'

'He's not. I don't know why you've got a bee in your bonnet about him.' But Topsy could feel her face burning, her eyes evading his direct look because she knew that she was insanely attracted to Dante.

'He's a player, Topsy. You couldn't handle him,' her brother-in-law told her in a tone of warning. 'At one stage a couple of years ago he was famous in banking circles for keeping three mistresses. One in New York, one in Milan and one in Tokyo.'

Topsy was appalled. '*Three*? Seriously?' she pressed, wide-eyed.

'Seriously, he's the equivalent of a suicide mission for a young woman from a sheltered background,' Mikhail delivered.

'Nothing's going on, Mikhail,' Topsy parried. 'I have a summer job with Dante's mother in a particularly beautiful part of the world. That's virtually all there is to this.'

Dante had or had had *three* mistresses. That sleazy little fact rattled round and round in Topsy's head throughout the drive back to the castle and left her feeling quite nauseous. What sort of a man went from one woman to another like that, treating them like interchangeable sexual utilities? And why did the X-rated imagery now assailing her overactive imagination actually wound and hurt? Why should it matter to her what he did in his bed? It wasn't as though she were planning to have an affair with him. She couldn't possibly be jealous of a man she barely knew. Yet neither could she doubt Mikhail's veracity because Kat's husband employed a highly trained investigative team. Through them, he had unparalleled access to background information about people he did business with and he was even more rigorous in checking out those who might offer a threat to members of his family.

While Topsy was lunching with Mikhail, Dante was entertaining an unexpected guest. Jerome St Charles, a member of the House of Lords and a widower, owned a house nearby where he often spent the summer with his adult children and their families. For a time, Dante had gone to school with Jerome's son, James, and as neighbours of long standing the two families still occasionally socialised. Once, Dante had even cherished the vague hope that his mother might return Jerome's obvious interest and admiration but nothing had come of it. Sad though it was in his view, his mother had remained impervious to male advances until Vittore came along.

'I'm sorry to drop in on you without an invite. I would've phoned first but I didn't know quite how to broach the subject,' Jerome told him, a troubled look on his patrician face as he pushed an uneasy hand through his thick grey hair in a nervous gesture. 'I'm afraid this is likely to be a rather embarrassing interview, but I'm fond of your mother and I felt I *had* to speak up and tell you what I know.'

Disconcerted as he was by that opening speech, Dante frowned at that reference to his parent and his light eyes narrowed with questioning intensity. 'I'm afraid I haven't a clue what you're talking about, Jerome.'

'It's this…' The older man settled a local newspaper down on the table beside the window.

Dante lifted it up and gazed down at a print photograph of his mother with Topsy standing in the background. The picture adorned an in-depth article about the charity to support women who had had miscarriages that his mother had started up about ten years earlier. 'What's wrong with it?'

'That pretty brunette working for your mother—I've...er...met her before,' Jerome divulged awkwardly. 'In London. I spent an evening with her... I...er...*paid* for her time.'

His green eyes darkening and cooling by several degrees, Dante stared back at him in unconcealed disbelief. 'Topsy? You *paid* for her time?'

Colour marking his cheekbones, the older man sighed. 'It's not quite as sordid as it sounds. She's not—as far as I know—a prostitute, but when I spent time with her she was available for the right price as an escort. I took her out to dinner one evening. I enjoy young attractive female company now and again and very pleasant she was too,' he acknowledged ruefully. 'But what's a girl like that doing working for your mother?'

'Let me get this straight…' Dante paused, his strong jaw line now set hard as granite, a tiny muscle tugging at the corner of his unsmiling mouth. 'When you met Topsy Marshall, she was working as an escort? And you *hired* her?'

Jerome nodded. 'We dined out. It was purely platonic. I had the pleasure of an attractive woman on my arm and she, of course, would've received a fee for her time.'

Dante gritted his even white teeth together, a combustible mix of anger and revulsion burning through him. Topsy was an escort; Topsy had worked as an escort! She had fooled him, he reflected rawly. Hadn't he been falling for the vulnerable ditzy act she was putting on? He was not easily shocked but the news that she had worked as an escort did shock him. Nevertheless he had complete trust in the older man, whom he had known all his life. Even though Jerome was embarrassed to admit that he had hired an escort, his sense of honour and his concern for Dante's mother had not allowed him to remain silent and Dante respected the sacrifice of dignity that the older man had made.

Jerome had barely departed before Dante received a call from his bodyguard telling him who Topsy had met up with in Florence. After what he had learned from Jerome he was just a little better prepared for that revelation. Mikhail Kusnirovich, the Russian oil oligarch, her ex-flame? Presumably, she was a former mistress, what else? Dante swallowed hard, knowing he no longer needed to wonder why she had been picked up by a limo or where her reputedly expensive diamond necklace had come from. Those expensive trappings told their own sleazy story. Such a dubious background did, however, make it seem highly unlikely that she had designs on Vittore, who had virtually no money of his own and no hope of any unless he got a divorce.

Had Topsy been summoned to the Russian's hotel suite in Florence simply for sex? Dante, his heart pounding, his hands clenched into fists, green eyes ablaze, paced his study in an ever-deepening rage. What else would she have been doing in a hotel suite but laying herself down on a bed? Mikhail Kusnirovich had made a booty call and she had answered it without the smallest protest. It could not get much more basic than that.

Yet he recalled her dismay during that phone call, his original suspicion that she was alarmed. Certainly, Kusnirovich was a man few women would dare to reject, a man of unsavoury reputation. *Che diavolo!* Was he making excuses for her now? She was a whore; what else could she be from such a background as Jerome had given him? Jerome might not have taken advantage of the situation but other men assuredly would have expected, even demanded, something a good deal less innocent than her company. Under no circumstances should such a Jezebel be working for his mother!

In a reflective mood, Topsy mounted the steps to the castle. Mikhail had not leant on her as heavily as she had feared, his mood doubtless softened by the delightful and surprising news that he was to become a father again without the necessity of Kat having to undergo another gruelling round of IVF treatment. Mikhail had also recognised that it was ridiculous for Topsy's sisters to fuss over her every move as much as they did and hopefully his more realistic attitude would eventually persuade Kat that her constant worrying about her youngest sibling was unnecessary.

Topsy was heading for the imposing main staircase when a door opened.

'I want a word with you in private,' Dante murmured curtly from the doorway.

'Maybe later. I have some stuff to do for your mother,' Topsy replied, shooting a lingering glance in his direction. *Three* mistresses, she was thinking helplessly. The surfeit of sex he was enjoying should surely have prevented him from demonstrating any interest in her. Yet it had not. His face was taut, faint colour edging his exotic cheekbones, his extraordinary eyes unusually bright below his winged brows. *So*

beautiful, she reflected before she could suppress and kill that dangerous thought.

'Now,' Dante ground out like a feudal king
demanding subservience.

Her chin lifting, Topsy stood her ground.
'But—'

'*Now!*' Dante thundered back at her in full
volume.

Topsy was so taken aback by the shattering
charge of anger he radiated that her feet automatically made the turn for her and she moved
towards him, her smooth brow furrowed with
concern. 'What's happened?'

CHAPTER FIVE

DANTE STEPPED BACK to allow her entry to the book-lined room and closed the door with an impatient hand. 'I've received some disturbing information about you.'

Topsy backed away from him towards the window. 'About...*me*?' she exclaimed in astonishment at the claim. 'What on earth are you talking about?'

'Jerome St Charles,' Dante shot back at her. 'He's an old friend and a neighbour.'

Topsy was aghast. That name struck her like a slap on the face for, of course, she hadn't forgotten that unforgettable evening, indeed wouldn't ever forget the indecent lengths she had been forced to go to before she could persuade her mother to give her the information she sought. It occurred to her at that moment that life could

be very random and unjust. What were the odds
of that man being an old friend and an actual
neighbour of the Leonetti family? How could she
possibly be so unlucky? On the other hand, she
had done nothing to be ashamed of with Jerome
and, unless the man had lied about the time they
had spent together, she had no need to defend
herself or make pointless excuses.

Dante strolled closer, his keen gaze sharp as
a laser beam on her tense and anxious face. 'I
see you recognise the name… Care to give me
an explanation?'

'I don't have to explain anything I do to you,'
Topsy countered without hesitation. 'As I said
before, you don't employ me, your mother does.'

'You will not distress my mother with any reference to this conversation,' Dante informed her
harshly, his contemptuous attitude patent. 'You
will make an excuse, possibly concerning a family problem, and tell her that you are sorry but
that you have to return to London immediately.'

Amber-brown eyes wide with wonder at that

demand, Topsy stared back at him. 'You're asking me to resign from my job and just go?'

'I'm not asking, I'm *telling* you to leave,' Dante ground out. 'You've worked as an escort. You're not the sort of woman I want working for my mother!'

'My goodness but you're prejudiced,' Topsy declared, her own temper rising. 'Astonishingly prejudiced and narrow-minded for a man in possession of *three* mistresses! I would've assumed that a live and let live mentality would be more appropriate in your circumstances.'

Dante froze where he stood, eyes widening slightly and then veiling below thick black lashes. Dark blood outlined his hard cheekbones while his firm mouth compressed into an unsmiling line. 'Where did you get that information from?'

Topsy flushed and made no reply. He hadn't denied it anyway. Maybe she shouldn't have thrown it but she had wanted to level the playing field. Why should she stand there being force fed his ethical objections when he himself was leading a far from moral life? 'You're a complete hypocrite,' she condemned.

'Mikhail Kusnirovich. He told you,' Dante guessed, struggling for the first time in many years to get a hold on what felt like an ungovernable rage. Dante never ever allowed himself to be out of control.

'If you've found out that I was meeting Mikhail in Florence, you've been spying on me,' Topsy gathered, fierce resentment lancing through her soft brown eyes and hardening them. 'What gives you the right to invade my private life?'

'I have the right to protect my mother from a woman likely to cause her distress and embarrassment. And a woman who has worked as an escort and who responds to booty calls from Mikhail Kusnirovich is not an acceptable employee on my terms!'

So inflamed with anger that she was on automatic pilot, Topsy stalked forward and lifted her arm. 'Don't you dare call me a whore or malign Mikhail!' she snapped back at him furiously.

A hand like an iron vice clamped round her

wrist to prevent her from delivering the slap she intended. 'Keep your hands to yourself,' Dante growled soft and low before dropping her fingers again in a gesture of scorn.

The vibration of his accented drawl seemed to hit a sensitive spot somewhere deep down inside Topsy and she quivered in treacherous response, eyes flying wide to connect with his as sensual shock engulfed her. Something about the way he looked at her called up a deep driven response within her. Regardless of how she felt about it, her wretched body was awakening and suddenly awash with sensations she would have done anything to deny. Her breasts were swelling, the heat of awareness surging to her feminine core. An intoxicating mix of shame and mortification gripped her that she could still be so susceptible to him. 'That wasn't what you were saying last night!' she launched back at him accusingly.

'Last night I didn't know that I was dealing with a practised little tart,' Dante fielded grimly.

'Whatever turns you on,' Topsy quipped unevenly, tensing at the straining tightness of her

nipples and the warm feeling of sensitivity pulsing like a taunt between her thighs. The atmosphere in the room was as thick and suffocating
as the quiet before a thunder storm. 'And although it is absolutely none of your business,
I was not acting like a whore with Mikhail. I
know his wife and his children well—I was having lunch with him and catching up on news.'

Dante dealt her an unimpressed appraisal. 'I
don't believe you.'

Topsy moved towards the door. 'That's your
prerogative.'

'You're not leaving…I haven't finished with
you yet,' Dante objected vehemently.

'But I've finished with you!' Topsy said
sharply, yanking the door wide to make her escape.

Before she could guess what he intended,
Dante wrenched the door from her grasp and
slammed it loudly shut again in her face. Shocked
by that very physical intervention, Topsy flipped
round and leant back against the door, needing
the temporary support of the solid wood against

her spine. She looked up into scorching green eyes that glittered like stars, so bright against his darker skin. He was seething and he couldn't hide it. 'Underneath the bankers' suit, you're not Mr Cool at all, are you?' she murmured in helpless fascination.

'Not when it comes to protecting my family,' Dante traded without apology.

'You're crowding me,' Topsy told him, because he was inside her space, way too close for comfort, the familiar scent of his hot male body distracting her when she could least afford to be distracted.

'Deal with it,' Dante grated unhelpfully.

'No, you deal with your temper,' Topsy advised, shooting straight from the hip. 'Exactly what did Jerome tell you about me?'

'That he hired you as an escort and you went out for a meal. He recognised you from a newspaper photo that was taken of you with my mother and decided that it was his duty to speak up.'

Topsy rolled her eyes in mockery, wishing he

would back off, wishing he weren't so domineeringly tall that he made her feel like a ridiculously undersized freak. It was one more way in which they were a poor match: her list of desirable male attributes specified a male no more than nine inches taller. It would be more comfortable for her to be with someone closer to her own size. Her sisters' husbands were *all* tall and whenever she disagreed with any of them she carefully kept her distance, having always understood that her diminutive height almost invited a bullying approach.

'You seem quite unconcerned by what Jerome told me,' Dante noted in a low gritty drawl. 'But my mother would be very much shocked.'

'I think Sofia would be shocked if she thought I'd slept with him, but not that I once dined out with him in a public place,' Topsy countered drily.

Dante stared down at her radiating frustration. 'That's not the point. He *paid* for your company.'

'And that's all he got. Don't make it sound like I acted like a hooker,' Topsy urged, big brown eyes increasingly defiant. 'I worked as an escort for only that *one* night.'

Dante finally took a step back and she breathed again, peeling her spine off the door, shrugging her taut shoulders to loosen their tension. 'Do you really think I'm going to believe that you only did it once?' he derided.

'You obviously want to think the worst and that's not being fair to me,' Topsy complained, sliding past him in a sudden movement that took him by surprise and walking back over to the window where there was too much space for him to corner her again. 'I went out with Jerome that night as a favour for someone. His usual companion was off sick and I was her replacement. It was totally above board and unworthy of your suspicions.'

'You worked as an escort. I'm quite sure it wasn't above board with *all* your clients,' Dante vented with a curled lip.

A sound of impatience escaped Topsy. 'You just don't listen, do you? Jerome is the only client I ever had because that evening was the only time I ever worked as an escort!' she snapped back in exasperation.

He shot her a look of wounding derision. 'You can't really expect me to believe that...'

'I went out with Jerome as a favour to my mother,' Topsy chose to admit, willing to tell him enough to satisfy him because she did not want to be forced to leave the castle just when she was beginning to get to know Vittore.

Dante frowned. 'Your mother?'

Topsy braced herself. 'My mother owns and runs an escort agency.'

'An escort agency?' Dante repeated in disbelief.

'There's nothing I can do about the way my mother chooses to make her living,' Topsy pointed out curtly. 'Unfortunately, one doesn't get to *choose* one's parents.'

Dante studied her in silence with caustic cool.

'Yes, I can already hear the wheels of your limited imagination cranking into motion,' Topsy told him sourly, her generous pink mouth thinning with annoyance. 'But no, I wasn't dragged up in a sordid household by a depraved mother. Relax—no sob story of that sort is about to come your way. I was raised in a perfectly respectable home by my eldest sister and I only got to know my mother again recently.'

'By the sound of it you should've kept your distance from her,' Dante commented, watching the tip of her tongue flicking out to moisten her full lower lip, angrily registering the stirring of arousal at his groin as perspiration dampened his skin. He only had to look at that luscious mouth and erotic fantasy took over.

Topsy was tense but the pulse of sexual awareness was like a monster running amok inside her body. She was remembering the glory of that hard sensual mouth smashing down on hers, the wonderfully solid feel of his hard, muscular power pinning her against that wall, the indescribable delight of his fingers touching her intimately and finally the waves of wickedly wanton pleasure that had followed. Her knees trembled, her breathing fracturing. 'Stop looking at me like that,' she warned him stiffly.

'You were telling me about your mother,' Dante reminded her thickly, picturing her on his desk, splayed open and ready for him. He knotted his hands into fists of restraint and breathed in deep and slow, struggling to put a lid on his overactive brain and the images flying up there.

'I needed some very important information from her,' Topsy volunteered after a perceptible hesitation. 'My sisters had warned me that she wasn't to be trusted but I knew what to expect from her and I was prepared. If you want to get on the right side of my mother you have to bribe her. She said that if I stepped in for the employee who was sick and spent the evening with Jerome in her place, she would give me the information I needed. We made a deal and she understands deals. I know she was hoping that I would agree to take on other clients and work for her as an escort afterwards but I never had any intention of doing that. I'm not that stupid...'

'What was the information?' Dante queried, wondering if he could believe anything she told him because of course she would try to vindicate herself in any way that she could. Naturally she would swear that she had only ever worked one evening as an escort and had no plans to do so ever again.

'That's private.' Topsy turned her face away from his hard appraisal, guilty colour mantling her cheeks as the movement made her long dark hair fall against her face and tumble in loose glossy curls round her tense shoulders. '*That*... isn't for sharing.'

Especially not with a man who would happily use that information to slam another nail in the coffin of his dislike for Vittore. Dante would become even more hostile if something embarrassing from Vittore's past were to surface to hurt or humiliate his mother.

'I refuse to believe that you only worked one night as an escort,' Dante drawled scornfully.

Topsy flipped back to face him. 'There's nothing I can do about that.'

'I do not keep three mistresses,' Dante told her in a roughened undertone, the denial wrenched from him without his seeming volition.

Topsy shrugged slim shoulders, face carefully nonchalant. 'It's nothing to me if you do.'

'You were angry about it, *gioia mia*. I could see it in your face.' Dante savoured his recollection of the moment. 'Like me, you don't share.'

'The rumour must've started somewhere,' Topsy replied, although she hadn't meant to say something so revealing and cursed her unruly tongue. Now he would think she was angling for an explanation of that story.

Dante closed the distance between them, resting his hands on her narrow shoulders. 'Once upon a time when I was very young and very randy I thought there was safety in numbers. Instead the combined demands of the three of them drove me crazy.'

His hands felt very heavy on her taut shoulders and her mouth had run dry because once again he had invaded her space. 'I wasn't jealous,' she told him vehemently, recognising that that was what he was driving at and furious at the suggestion.

'Neither was I, but the thought of you cavorting with Kusnirovich in that hotel suite outraged every skin cell in my body,' Dante confided huskily, long fingers spreading to smooth the tops of her arms. 'I can't stand the idea of another man touching you.'

'I'm not going to let you touch me,' Topsy pointed out half under her breath, her lungs less than efficient with him so close. And she wanted to touch him back so badly that it literally hurt to deny herself.

'Then say no now,' Dante advised.

'No...' Topsy said flatly.

'Louder and with more conviction,' Dante urged mockingly, setting her temper on fire.

'*No*, Dante *no*!' Topsy shouted back at him furiously, wishing he would learn how to take no for an answer.

A loud knock prefaced the abrupt opening of the door. Dante swung round with angry words on his lips, intending to rebuke the offender, only to see his stepfather standing in the doorway with a frown of indecision stamped on his face. 'I'm sorry to interrupt but I heard raised voices,' Vittore declared. 'Sofia was concerned when Topsy didn't come upstairs.'

Dante vented a soft laugh. 'We were arguing. I want to give her a driving lesson but she's not sure she's willing to trust me,' he murmured smoothly.

Taken aback by the speed with which he had come up with the excuse, Topsy blinked rapidly. 'Er…yes,' she contributed, not one half as smooth as him in a tight corner.

'If she doesn't wish to learn to drive she doesn't have to,' Vittore commented. 'It's not important.'

'I think it is,' Dante overruled. 'It would make her independent. She would be able to work much more efficiently if she could drive.'

'Right…OK, I'll take that on board,' Topsy promised, moving towards the door, desperate to make her escape and willing to use Vittore's arrival to facilitate it.

'And there's no time like the present,' Dante quipped, drawing level with her, one determined hand pressing lightly to the base of her spine to guide her across the hall. With the other he withdrew his cell phone and instructed someone to bring his mother's car out of the garage.

'It's a small and easily manoeuvred car,' he remarked, walking her outside into the sunshine. 'Perfect for the purpose.'

'I don't want to do this,' Topsy told him grittily. 'I don't like driving and I don't want you trying to teach me.'

'All you need to do is concentrate and you can't have got a doctorate in advanced maths without that ability,' Dante countered with assurance.

Topsy chewed her lower lip in vexation. She had never felt less like getting behind the wheel of a car. Her nerves were ragged after the row they had had, her emotions were still reeling from the shock of being called a whore and her temper remained in highly sensitive mode. Virtually everyone who had ever tried to teach her to drive had ended up shouting at her or at the very least raising their voice, convinced she wasn't listening properly to their directions. She was also convinced that domineering, impatient and far from even-tempered Dante was the last man alive to take on such a challenge.

'Climb in,' Dante urged, opening the door of the small hatchback with a flourish. 'Once you've got over your nerves, I'll hire an instructor to take charge. You have an entire estate of private roads here on which to practise.'

Perspiration beading her short upper lip, Topsy accepted the keys he passed her with a hand that already felt damp. He ran through every move she was to make first and then told her to start the car. 'Promise you won't shout,' she breathed before she put the key in the ignition.

'Of course I'm not going to shout,' Dante retorted drily. 'I'm not the excitable type.'

Well, that was a lie for a start, Topsy thought wryly. He had a really bad temper and when he touched her he was decidedly excitable and anything but cool or calm. In fact he already qualified as the most passionate male she had ever met.

'Are you planning to sit here doing nothing all afternoon?' Dante enquired drily.

He also had the patience of a jet plane forced to travel in the slow lane.

Topsy gazed out of the windscreen at the spacious cobbled courtyard and switched on the engine, which seemed very noisy in the rushing silence. A trickle of sweat ran down between her breasts.

'Run through your mental checklist first,' Dante advised.

Her mind was a blank and her teeth clenched together. 'I don't want to do this with you,' Topsy admitted starkly.

'Stop dramatising yourself—just get on with it!' Dante told her impatiently.

Thoroughly fed up with him and keen to get the experience over with, Topsy rammed the car into gear and hit the accelerator. The vehicle shot back so fast a startled gasp was wrenched from her. Dante shouted something and then there was a sickening crunch and a violent jolt that rattled every tooth in her head, the seat belt cutting into her midriff as it clamped tight.

'You total maniac!' Dante roared at her, leaping out of the car as though she had branded him with a burning torch.

Topsy switched off the engine and breathed in deep to ward off the nausea and the dizziness of shock. Detaching the seat belt, she opened the car door and shakily climbed out.

'You didn't even look in the mirror before you reversed!' Dante launched at her incredulously as he bent down to examine the damage to the bonnet of his precious Pagani Zonda.

'I wasn't planning to reverse... It's an unfamiliar car and I went into the wrong gear!' Topsy protested, folding her arms defensively while trying not to stare at the crunched-up metalwork that now marred the previously pristine paintwork of both vehicles.

Dante flung up his hands in a dramatic gesture. 'How could you accidentally go into reverse?'

'You were irritating the hell out of me...distracting me,' Topsy complained.

Brilliant green eyes targeted her. 'Oh, so now it's my fault, is it?'

'You knew I didn't want to get behind the wheel. I made it quite clear,' she argued. 'I'll go and apologise to your mother about her car.'

'Are you going to apologise to me about what you've done to *my* car?' Dante demanded.

Topsy couldn't bring herself to say sorry. The accident was his fault, absolutely his fault. 'You had an argument with me, called me horrible names and then demanded that I drive even though I made it clear that I didn't want to!' she condemned bitterly. 'So, if you ask me, you got what you deserve!'

Sofia handled the news of the damage to her car with complete aplomb, pointing out that she currently wasn't using it and that the local garage would soon have it fixed. Topsy insisted that she would pay for the repairs and apologised again. 'I'm afraid I don't get on very well with Dante,' she admitted.

A wry smile crossed his mother's mouth. 'My son is accustomed to calling the shots. I knew you would clash but don't let it worry you. I'm happy with the way you're handling everything for me.'

For the first time, Topsy asked to have her evening meal on a tray in her room. The prospect of facing Dante across the dinner table was too much for her. She knew she should have apologised. What had happened to her manners? But Dante brought out a side of her nature that she didn't recognise, provoking only an angry resentful response. He *had* called her a whore. How dared he? She didn't feel the least bit forgiving about that. One evening working as an escort did not make a woman a whore. Busying herself checking the guest list for the fancy-dress ball, Topsy made a note of jobs to be accomplished the following day after her trip to Florence with Vittore.

She felt guilty because going to Florence meant she would be taking most of the day off. Vittore worked part time as a financial advisor in the city and generally Topsy went sightseeing while she waited for him to finish and give her a lift back to the castle. Finally, recognising that her shattered nerves were keeping her stress level at an all-time high, she went for a bath to unwind.

When someone knocked on the door about an hour later, she stifled a yawn, knotted the sash of her wrap round her waist and went to answer it.

It was one of the maids carrying a beautiful bouquet of flowers already arranged in a crystal vase. 'For me?' Topsy commented in surprise, plucking the gift card from the foliage as the smiling maid settled the vase down on a table by the window.

Dante.

Topsy frowned in surprise, distrusting the gesture. Why would he send her flowers? What was he playing at? At this season the castle gardens were bursting with flowers and she could have picked an armful without anyone even noticing. Involuntarily she bent down, nostrils flaring on the intoxicating perfume of the roses, straightening with a jerk as yet another knock sounded on her bedroom door.

It was Dante, always, she suspected, quick to take advantage of any window of opportunity, any moment of weakness. He was very much a predator. She collided warily with his stunning emerald-green eyes. Colour warmed her cheeks and her mouth ran dry.

'May I come in?' he asked, smooth as silk, his self-discipline absolute, a faint smile even softening the hard, handsome lines of his lean dark features.

Even so, regardless of appearances, Dante was still recovering from the demeaning realisation that he had hit a hell of an own goal earlier that day. His temper had got the better of him and he still could not explain to his own satisfaction why that had happened. But he knew he should *not* have confronted Topsy about what Jerome had told him. He should have kept that information to himself and used it to his advantage because he could gain nothing by making her into an enemy.

In speaking up without logical consideration of what the consequences might be, he had not only made her hostile but also forced her to come up with the ultimate silly story in an effort to excuse her work as an escort. Could she really believe that he would swallow all that nonsense about her having traded a one-off evening as an escort in exchange for some indeterminate piece of information from her own mother? It seemed that she liked to play the poor exploited innocent and he was willing to play along with that to see where it led.

Topsy measured the risk of inviting Dante into her bedroom against the potential embarrassment of being seen trading words with him in her nightwear and slowly, reluctantly, stepped back to open the door wider, deeming discretion to be the wiser approach.

'I am sorry about your car,' she proffered on the better-late-than-never principle.

Dante expelled his breath on a sigh. 'I did force you into driving when you didn't want to. Understandably you were in the wrong mood.'

'You called me a whore,' Topsy reminded him bluntly. 'That was completely unacceptable.'

'Sadly, your work as an escort would make you unacceptable to many people. I'm not the only person around here who is prejudiced,' Dante pointed out steadily, noticing the way the fine silk of her wrap defined the pouting swells of her breasts and the luscious curve of her hips. His jaw line clenched in fierce denial of his burgeoning erection. 'But you are correct—working a while as an escort doesn't automatically make you a whore and I should never have called you one.'

'I spent one wretched evening working as an escort!' Topsy exclaimed, out of all patience at his judgemental attitude. 'It shouldn't make you think of me differently.'

'You can't be that naïve.'

As he was the first man to find out about that evening and his reaction was much worse than she had expected, she was beginning to think that she had been just that naïve. She frowned at the thought of how her sisters would have reacted to the news, knowing they would be furious with her, particularly when they had already warned her to be cautious around their mother. But only Odette had had the power to tell Topsy who her father really was and, hurt and bewildered by the discovery that the man she had always believed was her father was *not*, Topsy would have done almost anything for that knowledge.

'But maybe you are, *gioia mia*,' Dante breathed soft and low in continuance, gazing down at her with an intensity that burned.

'I always try to think the best of people,' Topsy declared, her breath shortening in her throat, the undertones in the atmosphere beginning to make her skin prickle with awareness.

'That's asking for trouble.'

'I don't want to look at the world that way!' Topsy protested vehemently.

A sardonic smile slashed Dante's stubborn mouth. 'But to protect yourself, you must,' he told her drily.

Looking up at his handsome features, Topsy was suddenly swamped by such a powerful tide of longing that she felt dizzy. He was gorgeous but so different from her in every way that she could not comprehend the terrifying strength of his appeal. It's just sexual attraction, a little voice said in the back of her head and for once that little voice was a comfort to her, for 'just sex' she could handle while the prospect of experiencing anything deeper unnerved her.

'You shouldn't be in here with me late at night,' Topsy said abruptly, recognising the danger of being alone with him in her bedroom, instinctively trying to protect herself. 'It'll give the staff the wrong idea about us.'

A surprisingly boyish grin slanted his beautifully shaped mouth. *'Non importa, bellissima mia.* I don't care about other people's opinions—'

'I'm not beautiful,' she told him thinly, questioning that endearment. 'But of course you're an Italian male and fully living up to the stereotype with your compliments.'

'I do think you're beautiful and I'm no stereotype.' Dante cradled her cheekbone, tilting her face up to better appraise eyes the colour of warm melted honey and the succulent pink mouth that haunted his dreams.

Topsy could feel her heart accelerating like

an express train on a downhill run and, even worse, the instant leap of anticipation that he alone could summon. 'Dante...*go,*' she urged hoarsely.

Instead Dante bent down and pulled her up against him. 'I want you.'

A tiny pulse flickered below her collarbone, her face taut with strain as she fought an urgent need to respond in kind. 'Put me down,' she told him stiffly.

'I'm not a rabid dog. I don't bite,' Dante teased, burying his mouth in the soft silky tangle of dark hair between her shoulder and neck and nuzzling her skin to kiss a trail up her slender throat, which made her writhe and gasp. '*Dio mio!* I *ache* for you!'

Her arms linked across his broad shoulders to steady herself. 'You only ache because I said no. If I'd said yes, you would already have lost interest,' she condemned.

Taken aback by that condemnation, Dante tumbled her down slowly on the bed. 'I'm not a teenager with a score card and I don't do one-night stands.'

'You're not my type,' Topsy argued shakily, looking up at him with wide, accusing eyes.

One knee on the bed, Dante bent down to mould a possessive hand to the swell of her breast, fingers withdrawing only to expertly massage the protuberant bud of her nipple through the fine covering of the silk. 'Your body says otherwise. As for the suits you don't like,' Dante mused lazily. 'Guess what? They come off!'

Her eyes softened at the teasing note in his voice, her attention arrested by the compelling smile he now wore. 'This isn't a game, Dante.'

'Isn't it?' A doubting ebony brow rose. 'What else can it be between us?'

And the spell of his charismatic presence broke in that same moment because what he said opposed her every thought and feeling and the shock of her recoil gave her the strength to muster her defences. In an abrupt movement, Topsy pulled away and rolled off the other side of the bed, standing up and folding her arms defensively. 'I don't play games, Dante. Please go.'

Dante studied her, taking in the wilful tilt of her chin, the blazing determination in her dark eyes, and wondered if that strength of character and continued resistance was what made her so powerfully attractive. When it came to women Dante very rarely met with a challenge. His clever brain coolly assessed the situation. He decided that on balance even if he hadn't got her into bed and gratified his lust, he was content that he had redressed the damage of their confrontation earlier. He might be back almost where he had started, but at least communication channels were open again.

Topsy got into bed, weak as a twig blown down in a storm: mentally and physically, he exhausted her. In the back of her mind she had been thinking that they could have an affair. He had worn her down, weakened her into thinking such a development could be acceptable. While it was true that she had come to Italy ready to extend her experience of men if the right opportunity offered, Dante Leonetti was so far off her scale of what was acceptable in a lover that he made her think more of disaster than opportunity.

An affair wasn't a game to her and she didn't want to get hurt. Instinct was already warning her that the confusion of emotions she experienced around Dante went dangerously beyond basic attraction. Possibly it was infatuation, she reasoned uneasily, but only children played with fire without fear of getting burned and Topsy didn't want to suffer so much as a scorch mark. So, on that score, Dante was strictly off limits.

CHAPTER SIX

VITTORE TOOK A last dissatisfied glance at the gold pendant. 'It's so plain,' he lamented, clearly longing for a more bold and sparkly design.

'I think Sofia will like it,' Topsy told him firmly.

Vittore nodded and proffered his credit card. 'We'll go for coffee before I head into the office,' he said, casting her a glance. 'My first appointment isn't until ten-thirty. What are you going to do?'

'My plans are fairly loose but I think I'll do the Uffizi again. My last visit felt rushed,' she confided.

'Do you get homesick for London?' Vittore asked her, having ordered coffee at a pavement café opposite the office he used.

'No, I'm enjoying the change of scene.' Topsy

hesitated, seeing her opening, moving to grab it. 'When were you last in London?'

'More than twenty years ago,' Vittore told her, looking reflective.

'Was it a holiday?' she prompted, sipping at her cappuccino.

'No. I moved to London to start up a business but it all went pear-shaped,' he volunteered wryly.

'What happened?' Topsy asked quietly.

'I fell in love with the wrong woman and she emptied my bank account,' Vittore admitted, giving her a rueful look when she could not hide her shock at that admission. 'That was the end of the affair and the end of my business venture. I came home to lick my wounds and never went back.'

Topsy was frowning. 'Did you tell the police?'

'No, I wrote it off to experience. I don't think the police *could* have helped me. After all, I trusted her and gave her free access to my account. What happened was my own fault. Back then I was still young and foolish,' he declared with a fatalistic shrug of his shoulders. 'Maturity does have some advantages.'

Topsy wanted so badly to ask if the woman concerned had been called Odette Taylor but if she mentioned her mother's name she would have to come clean and tell all and she wasn't ready to do that yet. Could the woman who had robbed Vittore be her mother? It was a depressing suspicion and only made the challenge of tackling the thorny mystery of her parentage more difficult, for if Odette had been the thief, Vittore would very probably be appalled to learn that he might have fathered a child with her. Already painfully aware of numerous occasions when her mother had been greedy and dishonest with money, Topsy had little difficulty picturing her avaricious parent in such a scenario. Odette had even admitted to her that she had chosen to lie and tell her polo player lover that *he* was the father of her youngest daughter because he had impressed her as a better financial bet than Vittore.

'You look very thoughtful,' Vittore quipped.

Topsy glanced up from her coffee cup and blinked in consternation at the tall male figure striding across the square towards them: it was Dante as she had never seen him before, his lean powerful thighs sheathed in tight-fitting faded denim, a blue-striped short-sleeved shirt casually open at his brown throat. Black hair ruffled in the slight breeze, strong face cool and calm, he looked breathtakingly beautiful to her stunned gaze. She moistened her lower lip with a nervous flick of her tongue. 'Dante's coming this way,' she warned the older man.

Vittore frowned, his air of relaxation vanishing. 'He didn't even mention that he was coming into town today.'

Topsy was covertly engaged in admiring the gloriously neat fit of Dante's jeans across his narrow hips and long muscular legs and in the midst of that wholly inappropriate appraisal drained her cappuccino in an effort to suppress her thundering pulses and an almost painful attack of self-consciousness. Soft pink highlighted her cheeks as Dante approached their table. 'I thought I'd find you here. According to my mother this is your favourite breakfast bar,' Dante remarked silkily.

'It is and your timing is excellent because I was about to abandon Topsy to keep an appointment,' Vittore remarked, turning his head to smile at Topsy. 'You could find no better guide to this city than Dante. Florence is the original home of the Leonetti Bank and where he embarked on his gilded career.'

'Is it really?' Topsy pushed away her cup and rose upright, keen to stress her independence, reluctant to be foisted on Dante like some hapless tourist in need of guidance and attention. She watched his eyes follow Vittore as he vanished through a door on the other side of the busy street.

'I didn't even know my stepfather *had* a job until today,' Dante commented.

'Your mother doesn't approve because it takes him away from her but he does only work four mornings a week,' she proffered, instinctively defensive on the older man's behalf. 'I would've thought you would be pleased that he makes the effort.'

'When I consider the size of my mother's income, it strikes me as a pointless demonstration of independence,' Dante said drily.

'Is financial worth your only marker of good character?' Topsy asked with spirit. 'Anyone with an ounce of sensitivity would see that Vittore is very well aware of his position and determined not to take advantage of it!'

His designer sun specs clasped in one hand, Dante gazed down at her, green eyes radiating irritation. 'Why are you defending him?'

'He adores your mother and he makes her happy,' Topsy countered in quiet reproof. 'I like him, I like both of them and it distresses your mother that you so obviously think so little of the man she chose to marry.'

A muscle pulled taut at the corner of his unsmiling mouth, his stunning green eyes silvering with cold anger at the reproof. '*Maledizione!* What right do you have to interfere in the private affairs of my family?' he ground out with disdain. 'Or even to express an opinion?'

Topsy paled and then reddened, feeling both embarrassed and irritated, knowing very well that she should have kept her thoughts to herself. The icy look of hauteur stamped on his face mortified her and she spun away to cross the square. A hand closed over her arm to hold her back.

'Where are you going?'

'The Uffizi.'

He sent her a derisive look. 'At this time of day? It will be a suffocating crush of tourists and you will only gain entry if you have a pre-arranged ticket.'

'I haven't,' she acknowledged ruefully.

'It would be a nightmare. Give up on the Uffizi and I promise I'll arrange a special pass for you some day so that you can browse in peace.' His eyes locked with hers and her tummy hollowed, her muscles pulling tight while her world rocked dizzily on its axis as if someone had given her a sudden violent shove. In the grip of that almost intoxicating sense of disassociation from planet earth Dante was all that mattered, filling her mind with insane thoughts that turned her inside out, filling her body with frighteningly familiar reactions she couldn't fight. She wanted him, *wanted* him in a way she had never wanted anyone before, craved him with every breath that she drew.

A slow, exultant smile slashed Dante's expressive mouth as he flipped down his sunglasses, closing her off from that visual connection that had made her entire body hum with excitement. She blinked, momentarily dazed by the clawing lash of desire unfulfilled and dropped her head, fighting for self-control and staring in surprise at the hand that now gripped hers.

'You haven't even told me what you're doing here,' she breathed unsteadily.

'My mother forgot to ask you to pick up her contact lens prescription,' he said prosaically.

'Oh…I should have remembered. She always has stuff for me to do here but I didn't want to wake her up so early to ask.' Topsy pushed her knuckles against her pounding brow as if she could force logical thought back into being again.

'This is the original home of the Leonetti Bank founded centuries ago by one of my ancestors.' Dante paused outside a tall sandstone building that bore all the hallmarks of ancient Florentine architecture. 'I started work here when I was twenty-one and a few years later we centralised operations in Milan and donated the building to the city to become a museum.'

'Twenty-one? You were young. Didn't you ever want to be something other than a banker?'

'What I would be was set in stone on the day of my birth,' Dante informed her drily. 'My father would have allowed nothing else and, fortunately for me, I inherited the Leonetti business gene and the affinity with numbers. You still haven't told me how you managed to spot the error on that document the other night.'

Topsy flushed. 'I could just see that it was wrong.'

'But you only saw that document for seconds.'

'I can't help it if my brain works like a computer sometimes,' she admitted soft and low, uneasy with the subject of the high IQ that had made her a gifted child and an even more gifted adult. 'Where are you taking me?'

He walked into the lively and very busy little medieval streets between Via Maggio and Piazza Pitti, the artisan quarter of workshops. It was like stepping back in time as she walked past studios displaying the wares of bookbinders, violin makers, metal workers, sculptors and cobblers. Topsy was enchanted because it was a taste of Renaissance Florence as only a local could have shown her. She had spent several mornings wandering round the city with a guidebook in a never-ending crowd of equally studious tourists until after a while the sights began to blur and intermingle and her brain went into overload mode.

In a design studio she chose a pretty enamelled photo frame for Kat in her sister's favourite colours and frowned in surprise when Dante attempted to pay for the purchase.

'It isn't for me, it's a gift for my eldest sister,' she commented as she politely refused to allow him to buy it for her.

He had more success when he bought her a lemon ice cream, so rich and creamy and smooth in texture that she loosed a helpless moan of delight as the icy concoction engulfed her taste buds. Dante lifted a napkin and dabbed at the tip of her nose and the corner of her mouth where ice-cream stains lingered. 'You're worse than a child for making a mess, *carissima mia.*'

Mesmerised by his flashing smile of amusement at her clumsiness, she looked up at him, amber eyes unusually serious. He *could* hurt her and only the night before that fear had held her back but now that pronounced caution felt more like an excuse for not living than truly living and she was regrouping, hungry for new experiences and wildly curious about him and what he could make her feel.

'We'll go for lunch now,' Dante decreed.

'I should be getting back to work,' Topsy protested.

'My mother isn't expecting you back. She has friends joining her for lunch,' he told her.

He walked her back to a Bugatti Veyron surrounded by a small crowd of admiring teenaged boys. He pressed a banknote into the hand of the tallest youth, thanked him for taking care of his car and tucked Topsy into the passenger seat.

'Where's the Pagani?' she finally asked stiffly.

'In a workshop for the foreseeable future.' Dante groaned out the admission and cast her a glimmering sidelong glance. 'You're a menace.'

'At least nobody was hurt,' Topsy parried, a flush on her cheeks. 'Where are we going for lunch?'

'You'll see.'

Her attention fell on a lean, powerful thigh encased in denim and she dragged it away again, struggling to get a grip on the weird, wild promptings assailing her. She might be curious but she wasn't foolish. Nothing was going to happen between her and Dante unless she allowed it to and she was in too much control to make that mistake, she told herself urgently.

Her head was all over the place; one minute she wanted him, the next she was telling herself that she had to resist him.

'So, where did you go with Vittore this morning?' Dante asked casually.

'He wanted my advice about a gift he's buying for your mother's birthday,' Topsy admitted, since she saw nothing wrong with sharing that.

'Why would he need your advice?'

'Because he always gets it wrong.'

'Wrong?' Dante pressed. 'How?'

'Vittore likes bling.'

A husky laugh of understanding unexpectedly sounded from Dante. 'I can see that that would be a problem.'

About half an hour later when they were in familiar countryside, he drove up a winding mountain road and, turning into a stony lane, he switched off the engine. When she looked at him in surprise, he shrugged and said lightly, 'I'm afraid we have to walk from here.'

Topsy climbed out into the sunshine and hung

over the door, enjoying the view of the forested slopes and the city now far in the distance. 'Where are we?'

'On the edge of the Leonetti estate.' Dante emerged from the boot gripping a substantial picnic basket and he tossed her a rug to carry.

Topsy gave him a startled glance. 'We're picnicking?'

'I think the food will be a cut above the usual picnic. Though I say it myself, my chef is unbeatable.'

Topsy anchored the rug uncertainly beneath her arm. 'I didn't think you were the picnicking type.'

'Blame yourself. I needed a good reason to put on jeans,' Dante quipped, striding off into the cover of the trees and leaving her to follow the rough trail through the long grass.

Her figure-hugging cotton dress rode up her thighs as she broke into a stride in an effort to keep up with him. She smoothed it back down, breathless in the heat, perspiration beading her brow. 'Wish you'd warned me. I'm not really dressed for the occasion.'

'I know but I wouldn't have missed that outfit for anything, *carissima mia*,' Dante confided. 'Clinging to your truly spectacular curves that dress is a show stopper.'

It was a grey stretchy cotton dress teamed with a colourful scarf but he made it sound like something else entirely and she flushed, unaccustomed to such masculine candour. Spectacular curves? She had long envied her siblings' whippet-slim frames. Clothes hung on her sisters as though they were elegant models while Topsy's infinitely fuller figure was much more of a challenge to dress.

'Why…a picnic?' Topsy asked, drawing level with him in a clearing below a spreading mature chestnut tree as broad in proportion as a bus. Beyond the clearing the ground fell away steeply into dense woods but the view over the quiet valley was amazing.

'I thought it would be more your style than a

trendy city lunch.' Setting the basket down, he took the rug from her and spread it.

The silence but for the birdsong crept round her like a cocoon. She kicked off her shoes and sat down on her knees, determined not to betray her nervous tension. 'Where are your bodyguards?' she asked abruptly.

'I gave them the day off. After all, I'm still on the estate and this was a last-minute decision that nobody else knows about.' Pouring the wine, he passed her a glass, the tips of his long elegant fingers briefly brushing hers. 'Drink up...relax.'

Relax? Topsy almost laughed at that impossibility. Being alone with a man who fascinated her to the degree that he did was deeply unnerving. She sipped the wine and let him pile a plate with a selection of the many delicacies he unpacked from the basket. She ate wafer-thin ham, dainty crostini snacks and Panzanella, a refreshing tomato salad. Lemon tart followed by a rich spicy slice of cake finished the meal. Having drained her second glass of wine, Topsy flopped down flat on her back with a sigh to gaze up through the sun-dappled canopy of leaves above her.

'I'll never move again,' she swore ruefully. 'I've never eaten as much at one sitting.'

'My chef will be flattered.'

A window of clarity briefly shone in her sunlight-and-wine-dazed mind. He had brought her into the woods to seduce her. He had even put on jeans. Topsy froze and then hurriedly sat up, deeming it unwise to lie horizontal like a sacrifice and encourage him. She collided with iridescent green eyes and a quiver of response shimmied through her. 'I know why you brought me here.'

Dante shifted fluidly closer. 'We both know why.'

'This is so *not* going to happen,' she warned him ruefully.

CHAPTER SEVEN

A RELUCTANT SMILE tugged at the corners of Dante's beautifully shaped mouth. 'But why not?'

Topsy sighed. 'When I was eighteen I made a list of exactly what I wanted from a man. I watched my sisters get involved with unsuitable men and getting hurt and I swore it would never happen to me.'

'What's on the list?' Dante prompted, silkily confident. 'I love a challenge.'

'Can you cook?' Topsy studied his face and the bemused frown forming there before sighing. 'I can't cook, so I decided I needed a guy who could.'

'I can provide a chef,' Dante pointed out with deadly seriousness. 'And obviously I can microwave stuff but I usually eat out when I'm working.'

'You can't beat the list, Dante. You just don't match. You're not modest or romantic or caring.'

'But I'm also not asking you to marry me,' Dante declared with staggering candour. 'And by the sound of it, your list was drawn up to road test a potential life partner.'

Topsy tilted her head to one side, long black waves sliding over one bare shoulder, dark eyes reflective because she had never thought of that angle before. 'You're right. You don't need to be Mr Perfect.'

'You choose me to have a good time in and out of bed, *gioia mia*,' Dante proposed silkily.

'No, you're definitely not modest,' Topsy commented with a helpless little laugh as she studied his face, marvelling that just looking at that precise arrangement of features could give her such an extraordinary thrill.

'Modest types lose boardroom battles,' Dante confided with immense assurance and leant forward to bridge the gap between them. 'And they probably lie about their performance in the bedroom.'

'How do I know you're not lying?' Topsy asked breathlessly because he was so close now a faint hint of citrusy cologne was tugging at her nostrils, instilling a powerful recollection of what it felt like when she was in his arms with his mouth on hers. An ache stirred deep down inside her and her tummy flipped.

'I aim to prove it.' Knotting one bronzed hand into the hair falling down her back, he eased her closer and sealed his sensual mouth to hers. It was like dying and being reborn in a burst of fireworks and celebration. Her awareness of her body shot from zero to overload in the space of seconds, every part of her reacting to the heat he generated.

Smouldering green eyes scanned her flushed face in the aftermath. 'Together we burn, *gioia mia*,' Dante savoured. Long fingers smoothed up over her taut ribcage to caress the swell of a rounded breast, ensuring that her breath shortened in her throat.

He reached for the hem of her dress and began to lift it and she literally froze at the threat of being naked in broad daylight. Suddenly she wanted lights she could switch off, a bed she could huddle in beneath a sheet.

'*Che cosa hai?* What's wrong?' he asked.

'Nothing's wrong!' Her throat convulsed on the denial as she struggled to get her nerves under control again. A certain amount of clothing had to come off, there was no getting round that requirement, she told herself. She closed her eyes, reached down to close her hands into her dress and tugged it up and off in one determined movement. It made her feel much better than the alternative of sitting there like a doll for him to undress; it made her feel that *she* was taking control. She glanced at him from below the rumpled mane of her hair, dark eyes provocative, her brain refusing to dwell on the reality that she was stripped down to a lacy bra and knickers.

'Time to take your shirt off,' Topsy told him instead.

His stunning eyes gleamed with amusement and he unbuttoned his shirt and shed it. The corrugated slab of his flat abdomen as he stretched took her breath away. He was beautifully built, hard muscles rippling below bronzed skin with his every movement. Her mouth ran dry as he unzipped his jeans and peeled them down with fluid ease, revealing black boxers that clung to narrow hips and a lean waist. She noticed, could not have avoided noticing, the bulge of his straining erection in the boxers and something clenched low inside her and she hurriedly glanced away, a more primal dart of apprehension infiltrating her. She was wondering if the first time would hurt and was realistic enough to assume that there would at least be some discomfort, but there was nothing she could do to avoid that rite of passage. Of course she could tell him she was a virgin but was afraid he would think she was some kind of freak to have stayed untouched until her age and the prospect of that made her cringe.

'Come here,' he husked, all warm tanned flesh and assurance, finding her mouth again, toying with her lips, stroking them apart, thrusting, in truth unleashing a repertoire of moves that disconcerted her because just kissing had never been so good before. Pulsing energy consumed her and she pushed against him, falling into those kisses and the delving of his tongue with shivering enthusiasm, marvelling that the feverish heat in her pelvis could be awakened by even that small intimacy.

'You have the most glorious breasts,' Dante murmured hungrily, moulding the high round globes with appreciative hands, tracing the tightly beaded tips and suckling the pointed peaks into the hot velvet of his mouth, parting her lips on a gasp and sending tiny arrows of need spearing continuously to her core. Almost as if she had spoken, when the hot, tight feeling between her thighs became unbearable, he tugged off her knickers and touched her where she most needed to be touched.

Her awareness of what was happening took a severe hit at that point as her hips squirmed and sensation overwhelmed every other response. His thumb circled her clitoris and a fingertip traced the sweet swollen tightness of her most private place. Her hips shifted and lifted, a whimper of sound torn from her as he explored. She could feel the wet readiness of her own body and the straining eagerness to reach a climax.

Dante shimmied down the length of her and used his mouth to tease her. Shock at the incredible intimacy of it rippled through her but the tide of pleasure he evoked was too great to withstand. The flick of his tongue across that tiny bundle of nerve endings made her cry out, excitement gathering that was out of her control. He drove her into a frenzy of need, her back arching, her body screaming for satisfaction by tightening and tightening until the wicked pleasure triumphed and an explosion of sensation overwhelmed her body as she reached the highest peak. In the aftermath her body crested down the slope of arousal on tiny aftershocks of earth-shattering delight.

She heard the crackle of foil, knew he was donning a condom and breathed in deep and slow, too shaken by what she had already experienced to feel her earlier apprehension. He rose high over her, pushing her legs over his shoulders and her eyes widened at the sensation of pressure as he pushed the broad thick head of his shaft into her tender flesh.

'You're very tight, *cara mia*,' he groaned. 'I'll stay in control, go slow.'

Topsy could feel herself being stretched, her inner muscles protesting his invasion and she shut her eyes and struggled to relax.

'You feel miraculous,' he breathed as he eased into her.

In the same moment as he pushed a little deeper she felt a burning sensation and then a sharp pain and she cried out, eyes flying wide, surprise and dismay etched there.

Dante froze. 'I hurt you?' She could see his shrewd green eyes deducing certain things she would have preferred him not to know.

'It's all right now…it's been a while,' she muttered dismissively, her face red and hot as fire.

Dante shifted his lean hips, sank slowly deeper and then withdrew and repeated the manoeuvre. A ripple of excitement gathered in her pelvis as her body clenched around him and he thrust deep with an appreciative groan. The delirious dark pleasure was engulfing her again by degrees, tightening her muscles, making her heart race, filling her with a flood of hunger. He slammed into her harder and faster, the all-consuming urgency of their entwined bodies enthralling her as another climax slowly, steadily began to build. The extremity of that orgasm when it came made her thrash and buck and cry out.

Afterwards, Topsy thought she would never move again because her body was in a blissful state of exhaustion. Dante dropped a kiss on the bridge of her nose and levered off her, releasing her from his weight.

'*Che diavolo!* You're bleeding!' he exclaimed.

And there and then she almost died of mortification, startled eyes flying wide on his shocked expression as she sat up and saw the smudge of blood on her thigh. She burned red from head to toe and folded her arms round her knees. 'It's nothing to worry about.'

'You were a virgin,' Dante breathed in audible disbelief, reprogramming his every former assumption about her.

'We don't need to do a post-mortem on it,' Topsy fielded.

'You should have told me!' Dante censured. 'I could have made more of an occasion out of it. If I'd known I wouldn't have taken you on a picnic rug in the woods.'

Embarrassed though she was, that had Topsy turning wondering eyes on him. 'You don't find it a turn-off?'

'I think it's the biggest turn-on I've ever had,' Dante told her, his keen gaze studying her with fascination. 'To know that at its most basic no other man has done what I've just done with you is extraordinarily exciting, *gioia mia.*'

In relief she leant forward and kissed him. He nibbled at her lower lip and then kissed her long and hard and before very long all talk ceased and they were making love again.

* * *

Topsy surfaced from a long much-needed nap to find that the sun was going down and she glanced at her watch in consternation. Dante was already dressed and the picnic packed away. 'You should have wakened me,' she complained.

'You must've needed the rest.'

Shy of him now, she flipped off the edge of the rug he must have tossed over her while she slept and concentrated on retrieving her clothing and getting into it fast. She felt downright astonished by what had transpired between them and the raw passion that had engulfed them had rewritten all that she thought she knew about herself. She hadn't known she had such a capacity for passion, indeed had often assumed she was more than a little cold in that department, for never before had she found it impossible to resist temptation. And Dante was the very essence of temptation on her terms. With him she was weak, she acknowledged. But was that necessarily a bad thing?

It was a fling, a little holiday fling, nothing

more serious. Neither of them was looking for or expecting anything more and on that basis they were a good match. As he had pointed out, he wasn't auditioning as potential husband material. And yet as she glanced at him when they reached the car again and he smiled, a feeling like trapped sunshine expanded inside her chest, making it feel tight. It was an infatuation, she told herself, responses heightened by the heat of the Italian sun and the taste of freedom she was enjoying. She was young and full of hormones, finally exploring a side of herself that had been on a leash for too long. What she was experiencing was normal, she reasoned frantically, not something she needed to worry about.

'You've gone so quiet. I'm used to you chattering,' Dante confided, shooting the car to a halt by the garages.

'I'm making a mental list of all the things I have to check before the ball next week.' Topsy hesitated and then forced herself to continue, 'Don't say anything about—'

'Of course I won't.'

Topsy's tension level dropped a little. 'If your mother or Vittore knew or guessed, it could make for an uncomfortable atmosphere,' she warned him.

She scrambled out of the car in haste, desperate to have a shower and relocate her poise. At that moment she was as awkward as a clumsy teenager around him and it galled her.

'Topsy...' His voice halted her as she sped across the courtyard towards the servants' entrance at the back of the castle.

Reluctantly, she turned, amber eyes welding to his lean, darkly handsome face and the sardonic expression he wore. 'Yes?'

'I have work to do as well. I'll see you later,' he told her smoothly.

Topsy fled, heart beating as fast as if she were sprinting. He could set her alight with one look, one word, even the rich accented timbre of his beautiful voice. It was as if she had succumbed to the worst possible addiction and the strength of it frightened her.

* * *

Dante walked into his study, a dark frown pleating his ebony brows. Topsy was always surprising him. Once he had realised just how inexperienced she was, he had feared she might be a little clingy—and he hated clingy women like poison—but she had taken off like a bat out of hell without even trying to instigate the expected fact-finding dialogue about where they were going and what they were doing. Her restraint had disconcerted him.

It was an affair, no big deal, he reflected impatiently, but the circumstances were not what he would've chosen. She was his mother's employee and, just as he had always ensured that his relationship with his staff at the bank remained strictly above board, he would not have chosen to become intimately involved with anyone working for his family. But then that was before he met Topsy and before he enjoyed a session of amazingly vibrant and satisfying sex that had only left him craving more. There was always an exception to the rule and he could not remember when he had last craved more of a woman so soon after having her.

In retrospect he could barely believe that he had cherished such sordid suspicions of her relationship with his stepfather and with Mikhail Kusnirovich. He was more taken aback by the acknowledgement that he had become so cynical about women that he had automatically distrusted the evidence of his own eyes and had decided, on no very strong evidence, that Topsy was a promiscuous little schemer up to no good. Well, she certainly wasn't promiscuous.

Topsy stood in the shower reliving his every touch and, with a frustrated groan, leant back against the cold tiled wall, angry with herself for being so susceptible. Where was her brain when she needed it? It was a physical infatuation, nothing more threatening and it would run its course soon enough.

Dante didn't join them for dinner and she was guiltily relieved when she heard that he was dining with his old friend, Marco, one of the local doctors, but she was also a tad irritated that he hadn't thought to tell her that he was going out. So, now was she trying to attach strings to him? He didn't belong to her; she didn't belong to him. Their lovemaking in the woods might never be repeated, she conceded, because it was perfectly possible that he might have decided that their intimacy was a bad idea.

On that thought her heart sank as if a giant stone had been attached to it and to give her thoughts a new direction she rang Kat and listened to her beloved sister burbling happily about what a wonderful surprise her latest pregnancy had proved. Kat rang off when Mikhail walked through the door of their London home. That was true love, Topsy reflected wryly, that desperate longing to reconnect after a parting, no matter how brief.

She was lying in bed around midnight reading an absorbing research paper on non-equilibrium dynamics and random matrices when her door opened, breaking her concentration. Closing the door, Dante strode towards her, his tall well-built physique bare but for a towel rather negligently looped round his lean hips. The very sight of him shook her up, her tummy flipping at the explosive effect of him in the flesh. He looked absolutely gorgeous. Her mouth opened but no sound came out.

'I warned you that I didn't do one-night stands,' he quipped, dropping the towel without an ounce of self-consciousness and sliding into bed beside her. He glanced at the article and raised a brow. 'Light reading?'

'One of my favourite fields,' she admitted.

'A doctorate in advanced maths,' Dante re-counted. 'You could have an incredible career in a bank.'

'I'm not particularly interested in quantitative finance or statistics,' Topsy told him, settling back against the pillows and striving to seem relaxed even though every nerve ending was jumping at his arrival. 'I think I'd like to go into theoretical research. I want to take my time about choosing where I work.'

Dante pressed his sensual mouth against the

remarkably sensitive slope between her neck and shoulder and she shivered violently. 'You *can't*,' she told him baldly.

Luxuriant black lashes lifted enquiringly on emerald-green eyes and her heart lurched.

Topsy turned to face him, her cheeks hot as fire. 'I can't…I'm…um…sore,' she confessed grudgingly. 'Seems there *is* a drawback to being a virgin. I'm off the menu for now.'

'I shouldn't have been so very greedy this afternoon, *gioia mia*.' Dante sighed.

Topsy rubbed her cheek over a broad bare shoulder smooth as golden satin, a small hand travelling across his pectoral muscles and wandering south, feeling whipcord muscles flex and tense every step of the way. 'That doesn't mean we can't do other things,' she told him with a hunger she couldn't hide, couldn't suppress, and simply couldn't deny.

He expelled his breath when she found him hot, hard and ready for her attentions. She loved touching him, literally could not bear to take her hands from him while she watched him respond to her every tentative caress, his inky lashes dropping lower over smouldering, wildly appreciative eyes.

'I might be a bit clumsy at this,' she warned him in advance.

'I'm all yours,' Dante breathed hoarsely, fingers gliding slowly through the silken fall of her hair where it lay across his thigh. 'Experiment all you like...'

And she did, revelling in the reactions he couldn't hide, triumphant only when he finally let go of his iron-clad self-control and shuddered and groaned his pleasure. Yet inexplicably it felt even better when afterwards he wrapped his arms round her and, even though he put out too much heat for comfort and took up too much room in her bed, she resisted the idea of waking him and sending him back to his own bedroom and could not understand why she wasn't being more sensible.

Over the breakfast table the next morning she studied his bold bronzed profile, remembering how she had made him feel, how he had made her feel, wondering when the infatuation would start to burn out and let her return to normal. She didn't like the out-of-control sensation he gave her. She liked to know exactly where she was going and what she was doing at all times.

After breakfast, Dante drove Topsy to a coffee morning for his mother's favourite charity, which was being held in a local town. It had been Sofia Leonetti's repeated experience of miscarriage that had first persuaded her to set up a local support group for fellow sufferers and the organisation had eventually become a charity. Topsy left Dante being fussed over by several middle-aged women and plied with coffee and cakes while she sped off to deliver the short speech Sofia had written for her. The older woman had already personally informed the committee members that she was standing down as chairwoman with immediate effect but Topsy gathered that Dante hadn't known because he studied her with frowning eyes when she referred to his mother's resignation.

'So, when are you planning to tell me what's *really* going on with my mother?' Dante enquired, tucking her back into his car.

Topsy directed a strained glance at him. 'What do you mean?'

'Don't play games with me,' Dante advised impatiently. 'My mother's not herself. Stepping down from the charity she struggled to build up is not normal behaviour for her. There's something badly wrong.'

'I don't know what you're talking about,' Topsy said woodenly, knowing it was not her place to reveal what Sofia preferred to keep secret while hoping that the older woman would decide to come clean soon.

'You're a lousy liar. I have sufficient respect for Vittore to assume that he wouldn't be walking around whistling if my mother were seriously ill,' Dante told her, strong jaw line hardening. 'For that reason alone I've kept quiet but I expect *more* from you.'

Topsy paled at that unexpected admission. 'Vittore and Sofia have private affairs about which I know nothing,' she pointed out uncomfortably.

'But you're remarkably cosy with them both. Don't think I haven't noticed that fact, *gioia mia*. And you may work for my mother but I expect your first loyalty to be to *me*.'

Topsy turned stunned eyes to his lean, hard-boned face. 'You can't be serious.'

Dante examined his expectations and realised to his surprise that he was deadly serious. His mother might pay her salary but Dante demanded one hundred per cent loyalty from Topsy when it came to anything that he considered to be important to him. He *expected* to be put first, he acknowledged, possibly he even took it for granted because women had always been so eager to please him, but he saw nothing wrong with his outlook.

'You're not being fair.'

'And you're not being honest or realistic,' Dante condemned without hesitation. 'Reverse our positions and ask yourself how you would feel if I was lying to you about your family. You know more than you're willing to admit.'

'We're having our first row,' Topsy commented stiffly.

'No, we're not,' Dante parried, skimming a forefinger down over her thigh in a teasing gesture. As he smoothly demonstrated his complete sexual power over her, a chill of apprehension assailed Topsy because he made her feel vulnerable. 'When I lose my temper you'll know about it.'

CHAPTER EIGHT

THE FOLLOWING EVENING, Dante gave Topsy a wonderful surprise by keeping his promise to arrange a tour of the Uffizi art gallery for her. He had secured tickets for a private viewing. Sofia surveyed Topsy's glowing face, her mouth tightening as her gaze briefly skimmed to her son's nonchalant expression. 'It'll be a very dressy occasion, Topsy. Those champagne viewings always are.'

Having piled her hair up on top of her head, Topsy dug a sleek black cocktail frock from her wardrobe and clasped her diamond necklace round her throat. Feet encased in fashionable and perilously high heels, she walked downstairs to join Dante.

'Between the hairstyle and the shoes, you've gained about a foot in height, *cara mia*,' Dante commented, the very epitome of designer elegance in a well-cut dinner jacket and narrow black trousers. Superbly elegant, he looked, as always, stunning.

'You suit diamonds,' he added, noting how the white-fire sparkle of the jewels seemed to reflect the brightness of her dark eyes.

Topsy involuntarily touched the diamonds at her throat. 'An eighteenth birthday present.'

'Kusnirovich?' Dante surmised.

'Yes.'

'Obviously you've known him a long time,' Dante commented, oddly irritated by the realisation and resisting an even stranger urge to tell her to take the necklace off. 'It looks like a very generous gift.'

Topsy simply nodded agreement, not wanting to say anything else and encourage more questions. Naturally he was curious about her friendship with Mikhail, who only socialised in the most exclusive circles, and while she didn't want to reveal the truth about her wealthy and powerful relatives neither did she want to lie to Dante.

The gilded event at the Uffizi was a true art lovers' dream. Beautifully dressed people sipping champagne strolled at their leisure through the rooms of magnificent artworks. There was no noise, no queues, no crush to struggle through and this time around she could even appreciate the splendid ornate interior of the building itself.

When she paused rapt before Raphael's Madonna of the Goldfinch, Dante remarked that she seemed to know exactly what she wanted to view.

'This is one of my sister's favourite paintings. She used to be an art restorer in a museum and, when I was growing up, she took me to all sorts of places to see wonderful pieces of art,' Topsy confided. 'She wanted to be sure that I got a really well-rounded education and she didn't quite trust my boarding school.'

'You attended boarding school?'

Topsy sent him an amused look as she paused in front of Caravaggio's Bacchus. 'I was a gifted child and, obviously, I was a scholarship girl. Kat could never have afforded the fees.'

'How gifted were you?' Dante prompted.

'I don't like talking about that, Dante,' she admitted quietly. 'I learn incredibly fast and I have a photographic memory for facts and figures. Let's leave it there.'

A tall beautiful brunette in pearls and black and white polka-dot silk strolled up to them and addressed Dante with the familiarity of an old friend. Her need to ignore Topsy's presence told Topsy all she needed to know about the brunette's true source of interest and she drifted off.

'Why on earth did you walk off?' Dante demanded ten minutes later when he finally ran her to ground in the Titian room.

'She was flirting with you and being rude to me. I don't waste my time with people like that,' Topsy told him without apology.

'We were lovers many years ago,' Dante admitted with a fluid shrug. 'She means nothing to me now.'

As soon I will mean nothing, Topsy's logic supplied, sending a wave of gooseflesh across her exposed skin. Her slim shoulders set back as if she was bracing herself for that day. She knew that their affair lacked the longevity gene. Soon, Dante would head back to the bank headquarters in Milan and Topsy, and having only agreed to work for Sofia for three months, she was returning to London at the end of the summer. He was a holiday fling, she told herself urgently, scanning his perfect profile in a hungry stolen glance. And the end of a holiday fling would sting, not *hurt*.

'That was an amazing experience,' Topsy assured him when she slid back into his car. 'I thank you from the bottom of my heart. Kat will be so envious when she hears that I attended a private viewing.'

'There's something I want to discuss with you,' Dante told her softly. 'I have to fly to Milan tomorrow for forty-eight hours—there's something of a crisis and I have a government minister to advise. I want you to come with me, *gioia mia*.'

Dismayed though she was at the prospect of

being without him for even that short length of time, Topsy was very practical. 'That's impossible. There's only three days to go to the fancy-dress ball. I can't possibly leave your mother to deal with any last-minute hitches that might arise.'

'I heard her say that you'd taken very little time off.'

'That's true but that was my choice and it doesn't mean I'm willing to leave her in the lurch. The ball is a huge amount of work and loads of little things could go wrong.'

'She has Vittore.'

Tensing at his persistence, Topsy shot him an angry look of reproach. 'You really don't like hearing the word no, do you? My answer is no, sorry…and thanks for asking…but *no*.'

'It should be yes,' Dante contradicted harshly, making no attempt to conceal his dissatisfaction with her decision.

'Arrogant…*much*?' Topsy quipped. 'You don't get to tell me what I should and shouldn't do.'

'*Non importa*…no matter,' he pronounced with

dismissive finality, wide, sensual mouth clenching into a hard line.

Well, at least she was seeing *all* his flaws, Topsy reflected unhappily as she lay alone in her bed for the first night that week. Dante was spoilt by having enjoyed too much attention from over-eager-to-please women. He should not be willing to put her in a difficult position with his mother when they could perfectly well cope with being apart for a mere forty-eight hours.

'Topsy…?'

In the act of crossing the hall the next morning to head into the dining room for breakfast, Topsy spun and raised an imperious questioning brow when Dante beckoned to her from his study doorway. She was still angry with him and it didn't help that he was so extraordinarily handsome in his formal dark suit teamed with a very chic fuchsia-pink shirt and black tie that one glimpse of him literally stole the breath from her lungs.

'A word before I leave?' he added expectantly.

Unimpressed, Topsy stalked towards him, outraged by his infuriating self-assurance. 'When you say, "Jump," I will never say, "How high?"' she swore in a sizzling undertone.

Instead of answering back, Dante swept her off her feet and up into his arms with the easy strength that always shook her. Linking her arms round his neck, he backed into the study and sealed her mouth to his in a passionately hungry kiss that jolted every skin cell in her treacherous body. 'You'll miss me,' he husked against the swollen contours of her lush mouth. 'I'll miss you.'

'But we'll live,' Topsy pointed out prosaically.

'For a woman who wants a romantic male that was a very unromantic comment,' Dante mocked, eyes dancing with amusement. 'You've brought fun back into my life, *cara mia*.'

He lowered her slowly and reluctantly to the floor again. Her fingers curled into fists by her side because for the first time in her life she wanted to hurl herself back into a man's arms but she wouldn't let herself behave like an adoring schoolgirl. Fun, *his* word and very revealing it was, she acknowledged grimly. Fun was never serious and never permanent. Fun was a fleeting thing of the moment and appreciated as such.

The next morning, Topsy had breakfast with Sofia in her private sitting room. With Vittore in Florence, the two women ran over last-minute changes to the seating arrangements for the many celebrities attending the dinner being held before the ball. Topsy noted the name of the woman seated beside Dante.

'Cosima Ruffini?' she repeated the name. 'Why does that name seem familiar?'

The older woman tensed. 'Perhaps you've seen it in a magazine. Cosima is a famous fashion model.'

Topsy nodded, wondering if Cosima was being placed beside Dante to entertain him. Was his mother playing cupid? And if that was the case, it was none of her business. Fun, she reminded herself doggedly, she and Dante were only having fun and temporary fun at that.

'Topsy…? May I be frank with you?' Sofia asked rather abruptly.

Topsy glanced up from the list, her mouth still crammed full of delicious melting croissant, and she nodded agreement, wondering what on earth her employer wanted to say.

'It's about Dante,' his mother volunteered. 'He's my son and I love him very much but I don't want you to get hurt.'

Topsy's croissant suddenly turned to sawdust in her mouth while colour rose hotly to her cheeks. She had thought that she and Dante were being so discreet that nobody would realise there was anything going on and, self-evidently, she had been fooling herself on that score.

'Dante doesn't seem to get involved in serious relationships. I worry that he may be what is nowadays called a commitment-phobe,' Sofia admitted uncomfortably. 'But he wasn't always like that.'

Topsy finally managed to swallow and clear her throat. 'Neither of us is looking for anything serious,' she hastened to declare.

Her companion lifted her chin and gave Topsy a measured look. 'I've seen the way you look at my son and it worries me.'

Topsy paled, not knowing how to answer that for she *knew* she was always looking at Dante, always mesmerically drawn to him when he was around, but wasn't that a physical pull rather than a mental one? She reddened, knowing the distinction was not one she could raise in present company. I only want him for his body would be a conversational killer, she reflected a little hysterically, because Sofia had taken her very much by surprise in opening the subject.

'Dante's wife used to look at him the same way,' the older woman told her softly.

Topsy frowned in disbelief. '*Wife?* His wife?' she repeated.

'I see he hasn't mentioned his marriage.' Sofia seemed unsurprised by Dante's oversight in that regard. 'Dante got married when he was twenty-one. Emilia and he virtually grew up together. She died within a year of their wedding—she walked in front of a car in Florence and she was killed instantly. Dante was inconsolable.'

A tragic experience of first love, Dante 'inconsolable'. That was a challenging image, which disconcerted Topsy for it had never occurred to her that he might be concealing such a past. 'He was very young when he married,' Topsy remarked abstractedly, thinking it typical that Mikhail had chosen to tell her about the three mistresses but not the tragedy that had preceded that change in Dante's private life. 'And no, you're right, he didn't discuss it with me.'

'Why would he have? It's a long time ago. I'm telling you now only because I don't want you to think too badly of my son. I doubt that he's ready for an exclusive relationship,' Sofia opined, 'but sometimes people do know instantly when they've met their perfect match...'

Topsy glanced up again. 'Do they?'

'It may have taken Vittore and I thirty years to finally get together but we first met and fell in love when we were sixteen years old,' Sofia divulged quietly.

Topsy was stunned by that information. 'Why did you break up?'

Sofia looked sad. 'Vittore was the son of the town drunk and I was the daughter of the most successful local businessman. My family would never have allowed us to be together. My father owed Dante's father a great deal of money and when I agreed to marry Aldo, the debt was written off.'

'That must've been horrible for you!' Topsy breathed in horror.

'It was but in those days you did as your parents told you.'

'So, how on earth did you meet Vittore again?'

Sofia grinned. 'I found him on the Internet and do you know? The minute I saw him it was like the thirty years hadn't happened and we didn't want to waste any more time,' she confided.

'What does Dante think of that story?' Topsy frowned. 'You haven't told him, have you? But it's so romantic, Sofia.'

'Dante is not a romantic man,' Sofia declared

ruefully. 'He would think us both even more foolish if he knew the truth.'

Touched by that story, Topsy took a while to get back to checking the seating arrangements. Her brain was teeming with busy thoughts. It was a shock to learn that Dante had once been married and that he had gone from losing the wife he loved to taking on three mistresses. Had he tried to bury his pain in rampant sex?

Whatever, Sofia's warning earlier was kindly meant even though Topsy had not needed it for she'd seen from the start that Dante was not interested in anything more than a fleeting affair. And she was content with that, wasn't she? She would return to London a lot less ignorant of men and look back on Dante as her first lover with fondness rather than regret. She had no other expectations, absolutely *none*, she assured herself doggedly, silencing and squashing the cry of pain deep down inside her. If she had accidentally managed to become a little too attached to him she would soon overcome that foolishness.

* * *

In Milan, Dante was frowning and tossing his phone on the desk. He had been candid with Cosima and, to be fair, she had matched his candour. Choice didn't come into the situation when the PR power of the ball would have a direct effect on the funds being raised. What was he supposed to say to Topsy? But then why was he worrying about saying anything? He reminded himself that Topsy had refused to accompany him to Milan. He didn't owe her any explanations, nor did he want to take their affair in a direction that implied that he wanted more. *Accidenti!* He didn't like complications and hated hassle, particularly with women. Keep it simple, he told himself impatiently. Saying nothing was wiser.

The night before the ball, Topsy agreed to join Gaetano for a drink in the village café when he rang. She was grateful for the distraction the invite gave because she had repeatedly and pointlessly revisited her decision not to go to Milan

with Dante and just as often she had told herself
that she would not rearrange her life, ignore her
safe boundaries or fall down on the job she was
doing simply for Dante's benefit. She had made
the right decision and she had no regrets, and in
the same way she wasn't sitting around waiting
for Dante to come home like faithful Penelope.
After all, he hadn't phoned her *once* since his
departure.

Dressed in a bright geometric print shift and
high wedge sandals, she skipped down the steps
and climbed into Gaetano's car.

'I'd have taken you for a meal but I don't want
my family to get the wrong idea and assume
we're dating,' the builder confided ruefully. 'Before you know where you are my mother will
get the baby albums out.'

'Your mamma already told me that you had
gorgeous curls as a baby,' Topsy told him with
a giggle.

'Besides, I hear you're seeing Dante,' Gaetano
commented.

Eyes wide, Topsy swivelled in her seat. 'Who told you that?'

'My kid brother saw you walking hand in hand through Florence,' Gaetano admitted. 'There's no such thing as privacy around here, particularly not when it comes to love lives. Gossip is the spice of life.'

Topsy seriously hoped that nobody knew about the picnic in the woods and went pink. 'Dante and I...well, we're just a casual thing.'

'I wouldn't want to tread on his toes,' Gaetano confided. 'When I phoned, I thought you'd say no to coming out.'

'I don't even know when Dante's due home,' Topsy admitted.

Gaetano asked her what she was wearing to the ball. 'It's a glorified maid's outfit,' she confided. 'Sofia wanted me to choose something fancy but basically I'm staff and she's the hostess, so I thought it made sense to choose something plain.'

'You could never look plain...'

In a white-hot rage shielded by formidable

cool, Dante focused on her vivid little face from across the street. Infuriatingly, she looked as though she was enjoying herself. He had been incredulous when he learned that she had gone out with another man when he was within an hour of coming home and he had been forced to sit through a session of his mother pontificating over whether or not Gaetano could get over his ex quickly enough to properly appreciate Topsy. As far as he was concerned, Topsy needed no other male appreciation. He was convinced that if he left her alone by the side of the road for five minutes he would find her surrounded by men when he came back. Topsy's *je ne sais quoi* sexiness and energy were a magnetic draw for the opposite sex.

Topsy very nearly fell off her chair when Dante strode into the café. Within seconds the proprietor was by his side and hurrying off to serve him. She studied Dante, hopelessly greedy for the sheer rush of seeing him again, her heart rate kicking up, a steady tension infiltrating her every muscle. As she met his remarkable green eyes her surroundings vanished into oblivion. It was a severe overreaction to his presence and she knew it was but she couldn't suppress it. A physical infatuation might have seized hold of her formerly controlled self, but her brain told her she could cope with it as long as she didn't let it take over entirely.

Gaetano was already cheerfully exchanging talk of the ball with Dante as he sat down, a glass of wine arriving magically fast at his elbow. Topsy glanced across the table at him, noting the heavy black lashes that concealed his eyes, the spectacular bone structure beneath his olive-toned skin. Dante had been married, she found herself thinking afresh. He had promised to love, honour and share with another woman and she had died and he had ended up alone. Alone but for the three mistresses, she reminded herself staunchly, keen not to idealise her image of him. Without warning he looked at her and a surge of unwelcome heat and awareness blossomed between her legs. Conscious her breasts were swelling and her nipples tightening, she sucked in a deep audible breath and soft pink warmed her cheeks.

'You won't mind if I take Topsy home,' Dante murmured to Gaetano.

'I've only had one drink,' Topsy objected. 'This is virtually my first break from work in two days.'

'I own a wine cellar. If you want to drink, you can do it with me.'

'And what cave did you emerge from?' Topsy asked sweetly. 'Obviously it was a very recent move.'

Beside her, Gaetano was trying not to laugh but Topsy wasn't amused. She didn't want Dante ordering her around. He didn't own her, he didn't have the right to dictate where she went and what she did and even if she had loved him she would have fought him to the death on that issue.

'*Madre di Dio*...OK, I should've phoned!' Dante ground out the grudging admission between even white teeth.

'Perhaps...' Topsy tossed back, refusing to give ground, her dark eyes veiled as she wondered if he had consciously decided *not* to phone while he was away, if indeed he was as set as she was on respecting the limits of their relationship. And if she was right in her suspicion, why was he behaving that way? And why change course to chase her down when she wasn't immediately available?

'*Venga qui*...come here,' Dante breathed in a driven undertone as he suddenly sprang to his feet, six feet plus inches of rippling impatience, extending a lean, elegant hand to pull her upright.

'See you tomorrow night,' Gaetano told her with an appreciative grin, saluting them both with his glass as Dante closed an arm round Topsy's slight shoulders.

'I hate it when you try and tell me what to do,' Topsy stretched up to mutter in Dante's ear as he walked her across the street to his car.

'It would have caused a scene if I'd just lifted you and carried you out,' Dante parried in a mild tone that suggested his determination to retrieve her at any cost was perfectly normal.

Inside the car she couldn't resist any more: she closed her fingers into his luxuriant black hair and dragged his beautiful mouth down to hers. Fireworks went off inside her, instant blazing, wildly colourful fireworks, and the connection left her weak. He pressed her back into the passenger seat. 'Next time, I'll phone,' he promised.

'Gaetano's only a friend.'

'I know. He's still hoping his ex's marriage breaks down, so that he can get her back,' Dante confided with a sardonic twist of his mouth.

They walked back into the castle. There was nobody about. 'I'm going to get changed,' Topsy murmured.

Dante scooped her up into his arms on the first landing and carried her up the next flight. 'We'll sleep in my room tonight.'

'But I didn't say.'

'I'm so hungry for you, *bella mia*. I didn't know two days could seem so long,' Dante groaned into her hair, the ache in his voice stirring something tender within her.

He settled her down on his huge four-poster

bed and she kicked off her shoes, reflecting that it was only a week since he had brought her there and she had walked out again, determined not to succumb. What had happened to that resolve, the strength of her original resistance? Already that night seemed like a lifetime ago. Dante lifted the house phone to order champagne.

'I don't need another drink,' she told him wryly. 'I only meant that I was enjoying getting out and having some company.'

'I'm company,' Dante told her very seriously as he took off his jacket, jerked loose his tie and embarked on his shirt buttons.

'No, you're my lover…that's different,' Topsy contended. 'Gaetano and I are friends.'

'And what are we?'

'Chance acquaintances having sex,' Topsy said a little painfully. 'We fell into this.'

'There's nothing wrong with that,' Dante reasoned, flipping her round to run down the zip on her dress. 'Pre-planning can make life boring.'

'Funnily enough, I would have said that you plan everything right down to the last detail.'

For a split second, Dante hesitated as he lifted her dress off over her head, his attention dwelling on the glorious swell of her breasts seguing down into her impossibly tiny waist and the voluptuous curve of her bottom. She was right: he usually did plan every move he made. But he hadn't planned on her. He was willing to admit that she was an anomaly in his life and didn't fit the usual mould but he wasn't yet ready to finish the affair. It would end when boredom set in as it always did and when his desire for her no longer drove him.

He caught her to him with impatient hands and his mouth burned on hers. Tasting him, savouring him, she shuddered as he unfastened her bra and stroked her achingly tender nipples. She hadn't expected the evening to end like this but she wanted him, *needed* him in a way she had never imagined she would ever need anyone and, even though that was scary, she could not deny herself the incredible exhilaration of being with him again. She pulled off his shirt, her hands relearning the hard masculine contours of his hair-roughened chest, trailing down to cup and tease his urgent erection, already imagining what it would feel like to have him inside her again.

'I never want to wait with you, *bella mia,*' Dante grated hungrily against her mouth, nipping at her full lower lip, making her whimper as he skated a fingertip across the damp silk of her knickers. 'And I don't believe you want to wait either.'

Topsy was trembling with desire, desperate for the passion he unleashed so naturally in her. Suddenly he was kissing her with the driving demand that always fired up her body, sending tiny snaking thrills of wicked anticipation through her. His caresses became a little rougher, just exactly what she craved at that instant because she was every bit as impatient as he was. His teeth grazed a pouting pink nipple as he wrenched her out of her last garment and a long finger speared into her unbearably sensitive depths. She cried out, helpless in the grip of the passionate need he had awakened.

He grabbed a condom, made use of it and

flipped her over onto her stomach, startling her. He pulled up her hips and thrust into her lush damp heat with exquisite force. He swore then in his own language. 'Did I hurt you?'

'Don't you dare stop!' she gasped, breathless with delight. Don't stop, don't stop, don't stop—it was like an unquenchable chant inside her head. Every nerve in her body responded to every plunge of his. Her inner muscles clenched around him, wild heat gathering at her core as he used his hand to stroke the most sensitive spot of all.

'Not going to stop,' he groaned, nipping at her shoulder with his teeth. 'I dreamt of doing this all night, having you over and over again until neither of us can move.'

His pagan rhythm filled her with excitement. Breathing was a challenge when the waves of pleasure were gathering intensity in her pelvis and her heart was hammering at an insane rate. As her body was overpowered by the wild convulsions of orgasm he gave a shout of completion and drove deep one last time. She writhed under him, her body flailing out of control as she reached her peak and lost herself in the exquisite ripples of pleasure.

'You were *so* worth waiting for,' Dante breathed with hoarse emphasis against her cheek as he held her close afterwards.

She tensed as a knock sounded on the door. 'That'll be the champagne.'

He vaulted off the bed, pulled up his trousers and zipped them. Shaken, she watched him, wanting him back in her arms again, struggling not to be embarrassed or ashamed that he hadn't even got completely undressed. The sweet spasms of her fully pleasured body were still quivering through her when he passed her a glass of champagne.

'What are we drinking to?' she whispered.

Shimmering green eyes rested on her. Her hair was wildly tumbled round her heart-shaped face, her luscious pink mouth slightly parted, one pouting breast on display, her creamy thighs exposed. His body hardened again and he gave her a shimmering brilliant smile. 'You look amazing. We're drinking to all the pleasure we can handle, *bella mia.*'

She reached out a hand and closed it over his. 'No, we won't be that selfish. We'll drink to staging a very, very successful fund-raiser tomorrow night,' she contradicted gently.

CHAPTER NINE

LATE AFTERNOON THE next day, Topsy was dealing with the reporters and photographers who had arrived to cover the ball and the many celebrities expected to attend.

'You're part of the household,' one of the women remarked thoughtfully, a redhead with a choppy haircut and bright dark eyes. 'Any titbits to offer on La Principessa and the Conte?'

'Yes, their romance is hot news right now,' another woman chimed in, looking hopeful.

'La Principessa? Sorry, I don't know who you're talking about,' Topsy admitted, knowing that there had been no princess listed among the guests that she could recall.

'Cosima Ruffini,' the redhead extended.

'I didn't know she was a princess.'

'A princess and a count. Those two go together

like salt and pepper. We were hoping there'd be an engagement tonight. It would be a great time to make the announcement.'

'Er...Mr Leonetti and the princess are dating?' Topsy prompted tightly, an odd whirring sound in her ears as though she had suddenly become light-headed, a surge of perspiration dampening her skin.

The redhead raised her brows. '*Dio mio*, you are out of touch and I can see *you* aren't going to be much help in the gossip department.'

'Dante and Cosima have been seeing each other for weeks,' the other woman informed her with visible impatience. 'In fact right now they're society's hottest new couple and we can't wait to see their outfits.'

Slowly and very painfully, Topsy could feel her facial muscles freezing while her stomach performed a sickening flip. At first she couldn't credit the enormity of the betrayal, could not bring herself to believe that Dante could possibly have done that to her but her companions were already exchanging chatter that made it clear that Dante and Cosima were in an acknowl-edged relationship, not one suggested by rumour alone. Shock hit Topsy as hard as an unexpected blow to the back of her skull and she felt hor-ribly ill and exposed. Clearly, Dante had been seeing another woman before Topsy even met him and he had had a fling with Topsy behind his girlfriend's back. Her sense of betrayal, guilt and hurt was so intense it felt like a knife blade sinking into her heart.

'Excuse me for a moment,' she muttered, even her voice fading as she sped off for the cloak-room and a much-needed moment of breathing space in which to collect her chaotic thoughts. In truth she wanted to run out of the castle front door and keep on running but that option was not open. Not only was it her responsibility to ensure that the ball ran smoothly, but she also had her pride. It might be battered but no way was she running away with her tail between her legs because a man had treated her badly! She would see out this nightmare evening to the fin-ish and depart with dignity.

When she emerged again, the photographers were already busily at work in the huge hall. A tall and very beautiful blonde clad in a very full turquoise satin and lace ensemble was regally posing, and even as Topsy hovered behind the crush surrounding the other woman Dante came downstairs and Topsy did not have to look hard to see the proof that her worst imaginings were true because the blonde and Dante were a matching pair, outfits co-ordinated in colour, fabric and design, something which must have been organised weeks earlier when the outfits were chosen. Dante was dressed up like Louis XIV, the French Sun King, and Cosima as one of his mistresses. Topsy searched his devastatingly handsome face, noting the tension etched there as Cosima rested a hand on his arm and leant closer to speak to him. *You bastard*, she thought in indescribable pain as the couple posed for pictures and Cosima made the most of the attention.

Dante had slept with Topsy the night before. She had been so desperately busy all day that she had not seen him since and had thought nothing of it. Now she truly understood why Sofia had warned her off her son, for clearly Sofia had known that there was another woman in Dante's life. An engagement was in the offing? Or had that suggestion been only journalistic excess? And what did it matter to her now anyway? After all, whatever happened now she was finished with Dante. There would be no coming back from such a revelation as his infidelity and deceit.

The celebrities were assembling for the meal and the catering staff, clad in plain brown medieval dresses and mobcaps, were moving round serving drinks. Reluctant to risk being mistaken for a waitress, Topsy had picked a similar dress in green and left off the mob cap supplied. As she checked the seating for the guests she discovered that a famous Italian actor had brought two female companions instead of the allocated one and she gave up her seat to one of the women without regret because the last thing she needed to do right then was share a table with Dante and his truly gorgeous girlfriend.

What an idiot she had been not to ask him if there was anyone else in his life! Why had she assumed that there was no competition? Why hadn't she smelled a rat the instant he came after her? As far as looks went she wasn't in the same league as Cosima Ruffini and only a body transplant could have remedied that hurtful reality. Cosima was a classic beauty.

Pain gripped Topsy as she watched Dante lead his girlfriend into dinner, the two of them effortlessly regal and impressive together. She was remembering him touching *her*, kissing *her*, holding *her* throughout the night and she sped off to convene with the caterers in the kitchen and escape the view of the hottest society couple in Italy surrounded by friends and admirers. She was sick with jealousy and the horrendous pain of betrayal and her own misjudgement, she acknowledged dully. She definitely wasn't as clever and cool as she had believed she was because her fun holiday fling had downshifted into a sleazy conclusion and now she would remember Dante with hatred rather than fondness.

* * *

The ballroom was beautifully decorated with flowers and the band was already playing when Sofia and Vittore entered to officially open the public event. Sofia, splendidly glamorous in crackling golden satin, rose behind the podium to give a short amusing speech, closely followed by Dante, who gave the latest figures for the fund along with the expected travel date for the little girl, Maria, suffering from leukaemia.

Thunderous applause and stamping feet greeted the good news and it was a couple of minutes before Topsy noticed the furore at the top table and rose from her chair in the corner to investigate. Sofia had fainted and Dante had lifted his mother into his arms to carry her out of the room with Vittore hurrying anxiously at his heels. Reluctant though she was to go anywhere near Dante, Topsy was fond of his mother and concerned about her and she followed the small procession into the drawing room where Dante laid his already recovering parent down on a sofa.

'What the hell's wrong with her?' Dante demanded of his hovering stepfather. 'You didn't seem surprised when she fainted.'

'Don't blame Vittore, Dante, it was very hot in there,' Sofia groaned, raising herself against the sofa arm with difficulty. 'This is my fault. I didn't want anyone to know until I had to tell them.'

'Tell them what?' Dante prompted tensely, his concern palpable. 'What's the matter with you? Are you ill?'

Well aware of what was about to be divulged, Topsy darted out of the room to fetch Sofia a reviving glass of water and by the time she returned the other couple's secret had finally been brought out into the open.

Dante was tellingly still staring at his mother in stunned disbelief. 'You're pregnant?' he was saying unevenly. *'Seriously?'*

'At least you didn't say, "at your age" but I know you have to be thinking it,' Sofia muttered waspishly. 'And no, it wasn't planned but we're over the moon about it now that it's happened.'

'Why on earth couldn't you simply tell me?' Dante demanded starkly as Topsy presented his mother with the glass of water.

'At first I thought it was the menopause. I never dreamt that I might still be able to conceive in my late forties,' Sofia confided ruefully. 'Of course I was overjoyed that I *had* but I was also very embarrassed about telling people, particularly because I've had several miscarriages. What would be the point of astonishing people with such an announcement if I was likely to miscarry *again*? And initially it did seem quite likely that this pregnancy wouldn't continue either.'

'But Sofia's been seeing a very good consultant and he advised her to rest as much as possible for what remained of her first trimester. She's doing very well now,' Vittore added, gripping his wife's hand as he settled down on the arm of the sofa beside her.

'That's why I scaled back my busy life to such an extent,' Dante's mother explained ruefully. 'I want this baby. I want this baby very much.'

'Yet you couldn't bring yourself to tell me?' Dante breathed tautly.

'I didn't want to worry you. This is a risky pregnancy,' Sofia conceded honestly. 'I knew you would remember how ill I was the last time I miscarried and I didn't want to put you through that again. I was also afraid that you would urge me to—'

'*Dio mio!* I'm not completely insensitive and would play no part in suggesting you terminate my own little brother or sister!' Dante shot back at her in a strained undertone. 'Yes, I'm afraid you will fall ill again but I can see how much this baby means to you both. All that I'm interested in is keeping you healthy and happy.'

'Thank you, Dante,' Vittore said awkwardly. 'I appreciate your generosity. I do not want Sofia to put herself at risk, I have never wanted that, but you understand that the dream of another child is very dear to her heart.'

Deeming her presence unnecessary, Topsy began to tiptoe tactfully back out of the room.

'Topsy…stop right there!' Dante raked at her

when she had not even realised that he had registered her. 'We need to talk.'

'I have nothing to say to you,' Topsy told him succinctly.

'Vittore and I will return to our table in a few minutes,' Sofia murmured, smiling tensely at the younger woman as her attention skimmed uneasily to her son's combative stance. 'Go ahead.'

Within seconds, Dante had crossed the room to Topsy's side, gritty tension etched into every line of his face. She stepped away from the guiding hand he put to her back, his proximity acting like a repellent on her because every time she looked at him she was remembering things she didn't want to remember, thinking thoughts she didn't want to think.

'We'll talk out here,' Dante breathed, pushing wide the door next to the drawing room. The lush plant-filled orangery with its highly decorative mosaic-tiled floor and indoor fountain had wide doors standing open onto the sunlit terrace beyond.

'What is there to say?' Topsy enquired curtly, fingernails biting sharp crescents into her palms as if pain could help her stay in full control.

'I've got plenty. For a start, why didn't you tell me that my mother was pregnant?' Dante demanded, sharply disconcerting her with that choice of topic and angle of attack. 'We're lovers. Why didn't you share that with me?'

We're lovers. That statement stung like a whiplash, reminding her only of her stupidity. He spoke as though nothing had changed but her world had fallen apart and she felt as if she were still stumbling round, struggling to stay upright in the midst of the debris. She was having to fight harder than she had ever fought in her life to stay in control. Nothing, she appreciated dimly, had ever really hurt her badly before; her sisters had protected her too well.

'I couldn't share any of it with you. Sofia wanted her condition kept a secret and it would have been wrong for me to interfere in a family matter. I only found out because of certain symptoms she had and her consultant's visits,' Topsy related flatly.

'My mother almost died the last time she was pregnant. I was fifteen years old and I'll never forget it.' Dante raked fingers through his luxuriant black hair, disordering it, his whole bearing illustrating that Sofia's illness had been a very disturbing experience for him. 'I am *very* concerned about her. You *should* have warned me.'

'I work for your mother. My first loyalty is to her and I respect other people's privacy,' Topsy parried in tart disagreement.

'You still should have told me. I was already very worried about her,' Dante revealed for the first time, pacing restively away from her. 'That's why I came home and stayed on. She had suddenly changed her whole way of life and I could see no good reason for it. Pregnancy never even occurred to me as a possibility. I was more afraid that Vittore might be having an affair.'

'*Vittore?*' Topsy exclaimed, astonishment bringing animation back to the frozen pallor of her heart-shaped face. 'You would have to be insane or blind to suspect him of infidelity. Vittore worships the ground your mother walks on!'

Dante swung back to her, anger brightening his brilliant green eyes. 'Yet *your* intimacy with him caused a good deal of local gossip!'

'I beg your pardon? My...*intimacy* with Vittore?' Topsy queried with sharp and sceptical distaste.

'Suddenly my mother dropped out of sight and Vittore was seen squiring a young beautiful girl round the countryside. Of course there was talk and suspicion!' Dante retorted crushingly. 'You're not that naïve.'

Topsy was feeling slightly sick as she registered what he was telling her and she cringed at the belated knowledge that she and Vittore had unwittingly become the target of unpleasant local gossip. 'You came back home solely because you thought I might be having an affair with your stepfather?' she questioned in disgust.

'When a young beauty and an older man are seen together too often, people assume the worst.'

Topsy was frowning, staring back at him with her chin raised. 'And you thought that too?' she pressed.

'I was worried that it was a possibility. Obviously my overriding desire was to protect my mother.'

'And yet even thinking that dreadful thing of me, you still tried to get me into bed with you,' she reasoned in shock at that truth.

'Better me than Vittore and, let's be honest, you *do* enjoy an unusually friendly relationship with Vittore.'

'Only because Sofia was unwell when I first started work here and the usual barriers came down once I guessed that she was pregnant. My sisters have been pregnant a half-dozen times in recent years and I'm an old hand at recognising the symptoms. I also spent a lot of time talking Vittore out of his frantic anxiety about your mother's health. That Vittore was feeling so upset and guilty about the situation put more of a burden on your mother,' Topsy pointed out grudgingly, refusing to admit that she had deliberately taken the opportunity to get closer to the older man for more devious reasons of her own. She had wanted to get to know Vittore and find out what kind of a man he was before she approached him with her belief that he could be her father.

Better me than Vittore. That crucial little phrase Dante had used bit deep into Topsy's self-esteem. 'Were you willing to sleep with me to take my attention off Vittore?' she asked bluntly.

At that thorny question, Dante compressed his wide, sensual mouth. 'That was the original plan but it swiftly became much more complicated because I was very strongly attracted to you on my own behalf.'

Her lip curled, her scorn at that claim uncon-cealed. Obviously he hadn't cared whether or not she got hurt in the process of his seduction. He had targeted her, wanting only to deflect her from his stepfather, and even though he thought that she might be a shameless slut encourag-ing the attentions of a married man he had *still* gone to bed with her. That did not say much for his morals, but then that could hardly come as a surprise to her, she reasoned wretchedly. He had betrayed both her trust and Cosima's.

But the sense of hurt Topsy was feeling was even greater because she had honestly believed that Dante had been as blindly, instinctively drawn to her from the outset as she had been to him. Now she was appreciating that that was far from the case. Dante had needed her to want him and had succeeded beyond his wildest dreams, plunging them into an affair that she suspected he would never have had with her under any other circumstances.

'You *planned* to seduce me,' Topsy condemned, stricken, fighting to keep the pain and resentment out of her not quite steady voice when she thought of how intoxicated she had been by his attention and how recklessly trusting and naïve to let her head be turned so easily. Not once had she stopped to think that it was more than a little unreal that such a gorgeous male should be in hot pursuit of her! Why hadn't that occurred to her sooner? After all, she did not possess her sisters' beauty. In fact she was distinctly ordinary in comparison, pretty on a good day and, in her own eyes, dumpy with her lack of height and pronounced curves on a bad one.

'By that stage I was already in over my head, *bella mia*,' Dante fielded in a raw undertone. 'Naturally once I realised you were a virgin I knew you were innocent of any involvement with Vittore and that the rumours about the two of you were mere gossip.'

'Don't call me your beauty. I'm not. Cosima is.' Topsy whirled away and stared at the humming-bird fountain fanning down a shower of sparkling water droplets to dapple the surface of the pool below. She was already cursing her unruly tongue for she had not wanted to confront him about Cosima. His relationship with the other woman was an unarguable fact and she was not going to ditch her pride to fight with him over that unhappy truth. Dante had wanted to distract her from Vittore and he had succeeded to a level she couldn't believe, even making her forget why she had come to Italy in the first place. She had come to Castello Leonetti solely to get to know the man she believed might be her father but since Dante entered the picture she had barely seen Vittore.

'It may look like that. Perhaps I should have mentioned her.'

'There's no perhaps about it!' Topsy hissed back at him as she spun back to face him, that casual comment cutting deep. 'I had a right to know that there was another woman in your life!'

'Let's not have this conversation here and now,' Dante urged in an undertone, eyes locked to her distraught face as if he couldn't look away. 'We'll discuss this when the ball is over.'

'Have you forgotten that I'm staying tonight and I'm planning to dance until dawn?' another voice interposed and Cosima Ruffini, looking every inch a princess in her grand turquoise ball gown, strolled deeper into the orangery to subject Topsy to a head-to-toe scornful assessment that left Topsy's cheeks burning. 'She's not your type at all. What could you possibly see in her?'

'Cosima,' Dante growled. 'We have an agreement.'

'And you're cheating,' Cosima pronounced dulcetly, smoky dark eyes hard as jet, scarlet lips pouting in challenge. 'You're with her when you're supposed to be with me and this place is swarming with reporters and photographers...'

As Cosima planted a possessive hand on Dante's arm Topsy walked away fast without another word. Nothing more needed to be said. Cosima evidently knew that Dante had not been faithful and did not seem upset. But then Cosima had mentioned that they had some sort of *agreement*. Thinking about what that agreement might encompass sent a shudder of very moral disgust travelling through Topsy. It was difficult to feel guilty about having slept with Cosima's man when Cosima was such a tough case and seemingly willing to overlook infidelity.

Topsy's cell phone vibrated in her pocket and she dug it out, pinning it to her ear.

'It's Kat. You have to come home immediately,' her sister relayed in a staccato burst.

'Something's happened and you can't be abroad and unprotected while it's going on. You'll be picked up early tomorrow morning. Can you pack up quickly? It *is* an emergency.'

Topsy's head was spinning, her mind buzzing like an angry wasp, concern building. 'Can't you just tell me what's happened?'

'Not over the phone. It's not a secure line,' Kat warned her. 'So, please don't say anything else.'

Topsy dug the phone back into her pocket. What had happened to which member of her family that could be called an emergency? A kidnapping? Her blood ran cold. It was a reasonable fear with her family circle. She went straight off to find Sofia, waiting until the older woman was free to tell her that a family crisis had arisen and she needed to return to London immediately. She wasn't quite sure that Dante's mother believed the excuse and didn't blame her because the call to come home was a case of perfect timing when Topsy could not face staying in Italy if it meant seeing Dante daily.

CHAPTER TEN

'I'LL BE VERY sad to see you leave,' Sofia confided. 'I've loved having you here, Topsy. You brighten my day and fit in so well with us. If only...' Her eyes veiling, the older woman clearly thought better of what she might have been about to say. 'Perhaps you'll come and visit when we've moved into our new home.'

'I would like that very much,' Topsy said warmly, bending down to enable Sofia to kiss her on both cheeks.

From the back of the room, Topsy watched Dante and Cosima glide round the dance floor while cameras flashed all around them, Cosima occasionally striking a glamorous pose and smiling to display pearly teeth. All the life seemed to be squeezed out of her heart and it was a leaden weight inside her chest, a constant nagging reminder of loss and pain. She wondered then when it had happened, when the fun fling had turned serious for her, serious enough to wound and cause lasting damage.

Last night she had wakened to find herself wrapped round Dante like a vine and she had shifted away until two arms very firmly retrieved her, welding her back into stirring connection with his hot body, refusing to allow her to keep her distance. And she had looked at him in the moonlight, her attention roaming over his superb bone structure, the twin dark fans of his lashes, his beautiful mouth softer and fuller in repose, and her heart had jumped as if she were on a Big Dipper ride of thrills and spills. Well, she had had the thrill, now she supposed she was in full spill mode and it was time to pay the piper for her idiocy. Few women, after all, would ever be able to claim that they had been seduced to keep them out of another man's bed. And when she had wanted Dante so badly, did she even have the right to call it seduction?

She watched Vittore sliding an arm round

Sofia, the warmth of his smile for his wife full of the love that Dante evidently couldn't read. She so desperately wanted to speak to Vittore before she left but she could not speak to him while he was with Sofia. And she might never receive another opportunity. Sofia had said she would invite her back to Italy but people often said such things in passing and it was doubtful that she had really meant it.

Topsy was on the way back from the kitchens, having sorted out a slight conflict between the caterers and the castle kitchen staff, when she saw the older man crossing the hall and seized her chance.

'Vittore?' she called. 'Could I have a word?'

He came to a halt with a look of surprise. 'Sofia told me you're leaving. It's very sudden.'

'Family crisis, I'm afraid. Could you give me five minutes to chat to you about something?' Topsy asked apprehensively.

'Of course. I'm sure Dante won't mind if we make use of his study.' Dark eyes frankly curious, Vittore pushed open the door.

'I have a request to make of you,' Topsy confided once they were safe from being overheard. 'But first I should tell you certain things. My mother's name is Odette Taylor.'

Vittore was stunned. He stiffened, that name clearly still familiar to him even after all the time that had passed.

'I suspected she might be the woman you were involved with all those years ago in London.' Topsy compressed her lips. 'She's not a kind or honest person and I won't pretend otherwise. I have virtually no contact with her.'

'I do not understand how you came to be working here. It cannot surely be a coincidence?' Vittore prompted, frowning with concern. 'The world is not that small.'

'It's not a coincidence.' And then Topsy got on with what she had to do and told him in as few words as possible about growing up with the belief that her father was Paolo Valdera and then discovering six years earlier that she was not his child.

'And what does…this have to do with me?'

Vittore asked, although she could see he was beginning to suspect by the pleat in his brow and the intent look in his unusually stern gaze.

'My mother lied about my father's identity because she believed Paolo was a better financial bet. She admitted that to me and a couple of months ago I had to do her a favour before she would finally tell me the name of the man she believes—'

'Odette told you that I was your father,' Vittore guessed, his astonishment unconcealed. 'Yes, of course I can see what way this conversation is going but I really don't think it is very likely.'

'And you could be right. There may be nothing in her claim at all because Odette does tell lies whenever it suits her to do so,' Topsy conceded, perspiration beading her short upper lip, embarrassment almost threatening to swallow her voice alive as she made that lowering admission yet again. 'But as you're the only lead I have I'd be grateful if you would agree to a DNA test so that we can both know for sure. I promise you that I don't want anything from you but information and that I will not discuss this with anyone else. I also appreciate that this is a particularly stressful time for you and I do not want you to tell Sofia and risk upsetting her in any way.'

'I would not take that risk.' Vittore shook his dark head slowly as though to clear it from the shock she had given him. 'I *can't* be your father! I understand that you want to know one way or the other but I do wish that you had come to me with this weeks ago.'

'I was trying to build up to it slowly but events have rather taken over instead and now I have to leave,' Topsy admitted ruefully. 'I really am sorry to bother you with this, especially if turns out to be another piece of my mother's nonsense.'

'For a DNA test you will need to give a sample. I suggest that you get that taken care of here before you leave and inform me of what arrangements have been made,' Vittore pointed out seriously. 'I will agree to the test to put your mind at rest and because I know that I was with your mother around the time of your conception and it is reasonable for you to ask.'

'Thank you. I really do appreciate it,' Topsy told him sincerely, her heart beating very up tempo as some of her nervous tension began to leak out of her again.

'And if there is anything in this, we will *definitely* be seeing you again,' the older man pointed out with a rueful, utterly charming smile, which was very much Topsy's smile had either of them but recognised it. 'One advantage you do have from my point of view, and please don't take this the wrong way—you bear very little resemblance to your mother in either looks or character.'

Topsy left him again in better spirits because he had dealt with her belief that he could be her father very kindly and he was willing to help, which was almost more than she had hoped for because she had feared he would angrily refuse her request. She went back to supervising the ball, chasing after first a mislaid purse and then a fur stole as some older guests began to depart while the younger ones made the most of the more contemporary music now being played and got up to throw themselves round the dance floor. It was an exhausting evening. Sofia and Vittore went upstairs about one in the morning and Dante took over as host with Cosima still by his side, at which point Topsy decided that she had done her duty and could retreat to her room to pack and check out the Internet for somewhere local where she could have a DNA sample taken.

When she entered her room, she turned the key in the lock. She doubted very much that Dante would approach her with Cosima staying under the same roof but she wasn't prepared to take the risk. She had nothing polite to say to him and screaming at him, revealing how very hurt she was, would only mortify what remained of her pride. She was grateful for the distraction of wondering what the crisis was in London that required her return and was much inclined to think it would prove to be a storm in a teacup.

She found a firm doing DNA testing on the

outskirts of Florence and noted down the address, emailing Vittore with the details. She would call in on the way to the airport tomorrow. That achieved, she dragged out her cases and began to pack, wishing she hadn't brought so much with her. After a quick shower she got into bed, rolled over and stuck her nose in the pillow next to hers, scenting the faint elusive aroma of Dante's citrusy aftershave and the husky smell that was purely *him*. Was he right this very minute making love to Cosima? Were women interchangeable to him? Had Topsy merely been a useful outlet for his high-voltage libido when Cosima was unavailable? Did Cosima take other lovers as well?

Topsy tossed and turned, unable to find the blessed oblivion that sleep would have given her. Her thoughts were all over the place but one thing she did know now: she had fallen hard for Dante, fallen madly in love for the first time in her life. That was why she was hurting so much, why the simple image of Dante in bed with Cosima literally tore her to shreds inside herself. Engulfed by pain, she closed her eyes tight, willing herself to calm down and be sensible. It was over and right from the beginning she had known it couldn't last, so what had changed? Loving him only meant that she had accidentally become more attached to him than she should have done, she reasoned feverishly. She would soon get over him again surely common sense would see to that? He had deceived her, betrayed her, used her, hurt her. He could never really have wanted her the way she wanted him and that knowledge cut the deepest of all.

'So what's the big emergency?' Topsy demanded as her sister Kat, a tall slender redhead, greeted her in the hall of her London home with outstretched arms as if she had been abroad for months rather than weeks.

A herd of little boys were dragging a dainty little girl out of the cloakroom where she had clearly been hiding with a teddy clutched to her chest. A sense of warmth and of coming home to where she was safe enclosed Topsy.

'If you give it to me, I won't tear its arm off!' Karim told his cousin Appollonia.

'If you hurt Rags I'll scream,' Emmie's daughter warned him, screwing up her face in challenge. 'And then you'll be in *so* much trouble.'

'If you touch her teddy, I'll shout,' Karim's father, Zahir, announced witheringly from a doorway, turning to say to the other man at his shoulder, 'I think it's time we packed them all off to bed.'

'It's too early for bed,' Karim protested vigorously, his little brother, Hamid, sucking his thumb sleepily to one side of him.

'Yes, it is, it is!' carolled his twin cousins, Dmitri and Stavros.

'I'm not going yet,' Kat's elder twin, Petyr, announced, looking very like his father as he folded his arms and took on an aggressive stance while his sister, Olga, played on the stairs.

Kat rounded on her children. 'When I say bed, you *go* without an argument!' she told Petyr and Olga firmly.

'Or I have to say it,' Mikhail breathed very quietly from the doorway.

'Come on now, children,' the resident nanny spoke from the top of the stairs.

Within the space of a minute all Topsy's little nephews and nieces had vanished and silence had fallen. In the interim her cell phone rang and she pulled it out, her heart thudding at an insane rate when she realised it was Dante. Part of her wanted to disconnect the call as she had been doing every time he tried to speak to her throughout the day she had spent travelling. He must have rung her a dozen times already and her nerves were worn down and this time it seemed easier just to answer it.

'Yes?'

'Why the hell have you gone back to London?' Dante thundered angrily down the line. 'Without even speaking to me? Without even giving me a chance? That has to be the craziest, most irrational thing you've ever done!'

'Dante? Why would I give you a chance after what you've done to me? I'll give you crazy, I'll give you irrational!' Topsy slammed back furiously, forgetting that she had an audience. 'I don't ever want to see you again. So, leave me alone and don't phone again!'

The awful silence around her finally pierced the shell of her utter misery. For the first time she wanted to cry and sob with the sheer frustration of the many emotions attacking her all at once but the combined power of her siblings' questioning stares stifled that desire.

'Petyr's getting very cheeky,' Mikhail complained with unexpected tact to his wife.

'He's a real chip off the old block, then,' Kat told her husband without sympathy.

'Karim started it,' Zahir's wife, Saffy, pointed out wryly.

'But we both know that my daughter loves getting your son worked up,' Saffy's twin, Emmie, countered uncomfortably. 'She deliberately teases him.'

'No matter. Royalty has to learn self-discipline,' Zahir spelled out wryly. 'And Karim is too inclined to get bossy with little girls.'

Topsy gave her twin sisters an awkward hug, avoiding the looks that told her they now had lots of questions to ask, and said, 'Does anyone care to tell me why I had to come home so suddenly?'

Every pair of eyes in the room seemed to meet in mute discomfiture and a heavy silence fell in response to her question.

'It's Odette,' Saffy advanced reluctantly.

'She's been arrested,' Emmie chimed in behind her twin.

'Arrested?' Topsy exclaimed in horror.

'Accused of living off immoral earnings from her escort agency,' her brother-in-law Zahir supplied grimly.

Topsy sank down shakily into a seat, appalled by the news, well aware of how much embarrassment such a case being taken to court could cause her relatives. As the ruling King and Queen of a conservative Gulf state, possibly Zahir and his family had the most to fear from being publicly linked to Saffy's mother.

'I couldn't care less what happens to her,' Emmie's husband, Bastian Christou, admitted with unnerving cool. 'After what she did to my wife, it's past time she got her comeuppance and if it takes the law to do it, so be it.'

'But in the meantime we don't want our families or our reputations smeared by her dodgy lifestyle,' Mikhail pronounced in direct disagreement.

Topsy said nothing while the three men in the room began to argue about how best to deal with Odette's arrest. Her sisters clumped together exchanging grimaces until finally the broad terms of a reluctant agreement were thrashed out between the men. They would hire a good legal team to represent Odette in court but in no other way would any of them get more closely involved.

Topsy tried to imagine how Dante would have reacted to the news that her mother was going to be hauled up in court to answer a charge of living off the proceeds of prostitution and she shuddered sickly, grateful he would never know. Her sisters weren't saying anything and neither was she and, sadly, she understood why: they were one and all ashamed to death of Odette and the dubious way in which she made her living. Several attempts had already been made to persuade her mother to sell her business but Odette had demanded so much money in compensation that even her wealthy sons-in-law had baulked, believing that she would continue trying to blackmail them.

'Dante?' Mikhail queried softly to one side of Topsy, his approach having gone unnoticed by her in the state she was in. 'Was that Dante Leonetti phoning you?'

Topsy wrapped her arms round herself, suddenly cold, suddenly exhausted by the mental and physical stress of the past forty-eight hours. In silence she nodded.

'But I warned you about him,' her Russian brother-in-law reminded her.

'It was too late by then,' she muttered, wondering at what exact hour her fate had been cast. The first time she rested her eyes on that lean, devastatingly good-looking face of Dante's? The first kiss? The first time he held her hand?

'But by the sound of it, it's over now,' Kat commented, crossing the room to close a supportive arm round her youngest sister. 'What did he do to you?'

Saffy was the next to move closer. *'Spill,'* she urged.

But Topsy couldn't spill, couldn't bring herself to admit that Dante had had another woman all along. Blanking out her sisters' frustration over her refusal to talk about Dante, she confessed to suspecting that Vittore was her father instead and told her sisters about the DNA testing to take place. That provided a comfortable alternative to discussing Dante, and after dinner when Odette was the main topic of conversation, Topsy took refuge in her bedroom. She needed her own place, she really did need a corner of her own, she conceded ruefully, and she texted Saffy to ask if the couple's town house was free or if they were staying there on this visit. Generally when there was a family conclave, everyone stayed with Mikhail and Kat because they lived in an enormous house. Saffy confirmed that their house would be free but urged her to stay on with the family for company for a few more days.

Three days later, when Topsy was convinced that she was dying from the inside out in the slowest and most painful of ways, Dante showed up at Kat and Mikhail's on an evening when they were entertaining. She had tried so hard not to think about Dante, not to keep on going over the same old pointless ground inside her head. It was done and dusted, finished with no need of a post-mortem to drag her spirits down further. That constant mantra kept her together until above the sound of the jazz pianist playing she heard the sound of raised voices from the hall and then the noisy crash of breaking china. Taken aback, she followed Kat and Mikhail to the doorway.

Four men were engaged in a physical fight in the hall, two of them Mikhail's security guards and the other two she recognised from Italy as working for Dante.

'Dante...' she whispered in astonishment, seeing his tall, powerful figure poised by the front door, which still stood wide open on the night air. And every feeling and sensation she had tried to deny and suppress came flooding back to her in a violent shameful wave. In his charcoal-grey suit, he looked amazing: cool, sophisticated, wonderfully handsome, all the gifts that she had told herself all her adult life were superficial and unimportant. But that awareness did not prevent her from responding to Dante's pure physical charisma.

In a thunderous burst of Russian, Mikhail intervened in the free-for-all of angry men and told his bodyguards to take the fight outside before saying in English to Dante, 'Topsy doesn't want to see you.'

But Topsy *did* want to see Dante; she wanted to see him and speak to him so badly that the prospect of him leaving again hurt and that sudden burst of lowering self-knowledge slashed her pride to ribbons.

'I'm sorry about the fight,' Dante said drily. 'One of your men took a swing at me when I became insistent on entering and one of mine took offence.'

'You can't see Topsy,' Mikhail retorted harshly.

'I won't let you tell me no,' Dante countered without hesitation, striding forward like man with a death wish.

Topsy leapt into the space between the two men. Mikhail was as tall as he was wide and much more heavily built than Dante. She registered that she could not bear to see Dante physically hurt. She knew she should *want* to see him smashed through the nearest wall and slung from the house, but for some peculiar reason she didn't.

'Don't you dare lay a finger on him!' she warned Mikhail instead.

'Topsy!' Kat interposed in shaken reproach.

'I do not require your protection, Topsy,' Dante

growled from behind her as he carefully set her to one side of him.

'Actually, you do,' Mikhail informed him grimly. 'Anyone who hurts or harms Topsy is liable to get damaged here.'

Zahir's handsome and charming kid brother, Prince Akram, walked over and grabbed Topsy's hand without ceremony. 'Let your family handle this,' he advised. 'Let's go and have some supper.'

'And who the hell are you?' Dante suddenly roared at poor Akram like a lion watching someone stroll in to try and steal his prey.

'Exactly what have you got to be all jealous and possessive about?' Topsy roared back at him, losing her own temper with an abruptness that startled her and everyone around her. 'You're the one with the girlfriend you didn't mention!'

'*Kick* him out, Mikhail!' Kat snapped suddenly.

'I do not have a girlfriend. I am not involved with Cosima,' Dante spelled out between clenched teeth. 'Now will you listen to me?'

'I was kind of looking forward to kicking you,' Mikhail told him cheerfully.

'Is your family always like this?' Dante groaned, his emerald-green eyes almost radiant with raw-edged tension in his handsome face. 'Is nothing private?'

'Very little, I'm afraid,' Zahir dropped in gently. 'And cross one and you cross them all.'

'I do want to hear what you have to say,' Topsy admitted tightly, her eyes suddenly stinging with tears because she had thought she would never ever see Dante again and seeing him in Kat's home so unexpectedly was extremely disconcerting and had knocked her right off balance. Had he followed her to London? Or had he been coming to London anyway on banking business? And what did it matter either way? Couldn't she even control her own brain any more?

'We'll go back to my hotel.'

Saffy dug a set of keys from her clutch bag and dropped them into Topsy's hand. 'Use our place. It's more private.'

'You can't just walk out of here with that man,'

Kat argued worriedly. 'He's got a bad temper. He looked at Akram as if he was going to hit him. Suppose he loses that temper with Topsy?'

A pained light entered Dante's eyes. 'I am not going to lose my temper or hit *anyone*.'

'You lost your temper when I smashed your car!' Topsy reminded him resentfully.

Mikhail closed a comforting arm gently round his wife's taut shoulders. 'Topsy's all grown up, Kat. It's time to cut her loose.'

'You've got the family from hell,' Dante told her darkly outside the front door. 'I've never met a more interfering bunch of people.'

'But they love me a lot,' Topsy replied ruefully. 'I'm lucky to have them.'

'Not your mother though. I saw an article about her in a tabloid newspaper,' he admitted curtly, a hand at her elbow as he guided her out to the limo parked outside. 'It was only thanks to that article that I was able to track you down. The sole address my mother had for you was your mother's apartment, which is, of course, empty.

I assume that was another attempt to cover up your connections with your family.'

'You read about Mum?' Topsy felt totally humiliated by that admission. She had deliberately not read any of the newspaper reports about their mother's arrest. She knew that studying highly coloured revelations about Odette's turbulent life would only upset her because Kat was doing exactly that and had already been in tears over the stories several times. Mikhail had begged his wife not to read the newspapers, pointing out that the inaccurate articles were written to shock, rather than inform, and that Odette's plight would only attract tabloid interest for a few days at most. Fortunately nothing more was likely to appear in the media until the older woman was tried in court.

'Yes,' Dante confirmed with a forbidding jerk of his stubborn jaw. 'I thought I did badly in the parental lottery but clearly you didn't do very much better.'

'*Your* mother's lovely. How can you say that?' she demanded in bewilderment, sliding into the limousine and leaning forward to give his driver the address of Zahir and Saffy's house.

As he buzzed the partition shut between the front and the back of the car Dante's jaw line clenched hard, his eyes glinting like crushed green ice below the fringe of his black lashes. 'I wasn't referring to her. My father was a violent man, who used my mother like a punch bag,' he confessed, every word seemingly wrenched from him against his will. 'Worst of all, he got away with it because she was too scared of him to report him to the police and when he developed a brain tumour she nursed him right to the end.'

'Couldn't you have done something to help her?'

'I tried. She was terrified of anyone finding out about what went on in our home. She was deeply ashamed of it and blamed herself for everything that was happening.'

'How could she do that?'

'She said she never loved him and he always knew it and hated her for it.'

'I think she was in love with Vittore when she married your father. It wasn't as though she wanted to marry him, so I suppose he got what he deserved when he used his power and influence to get the girl he wanted.'

Dante frowned at her in bemusement. 'Vittore? How could she have been in love with Vittore when my father married her when she was only seventeen?'

And at that point Topsy realised she had spoken out of turn, revealing facts Dante had not been told. At the same time, she felt he should know that story to understand the strength of the ties between his mother and his stepfather. That conviction in mind, she shared what she had learned.

Dante was very much disconcerted. 'I didn't know she knew him when she was young. Why didn't she tell me? They got married so fast. I wouldn't have been as concerned had I known.'

'Well, you know now,' Topsy responded, thinking that in some ways Sofia and Vittore had contributed unfairly to Dante's reserved response to their marriage. Greater candour could well have changed his attitude.

'It's not important now,' Dante breathed in sudden dismissal. 'But the reason my mother almost died during that last pregnancy with my father was because his violence had caused internal bleeding...'

Topsy grimaced in silence.

'Soon after that *I* tried to protect her from him and I hit him but, unluckily for me, I was a weedy teenager, who didn't grow big and strong until I was much older,' he volunteered tight-mouthed.

She wondered if that was the time he had been found badly beaten up by the side of the road and her heart squeezed, the awareness that he had grown up in a profoundly disturbed and unhappy home somehow punching a small hole in the wall of her angry resistance to him. She couldn't forgive him for Cosima and still couldn't comprehend why he had come to London, for what could he possibly hope to achieve by seeing her again?

Yet she felt better for understanding him a little more and could only wonder if his childhood experience of violence and his parents' unhappy marriage had damaged his ability to deeply care for someone else. And then she remembered, with a sense of utter foolishness and sheepish self-loathing, that he *had* married a woman at the age of twenty-one. After that recollection she could only question why on earth her brain should be set on trying to find excuses for *his* inexcusable behaviour!

She unlocked the door of the town house and stepped inside. Lamps were already lit and the temperature made it clear that the heating was on: Saffy must have contacted their caretaker/housekeeper to forewarn her of their arrival.

A gas fire flamed in the grate and Dante examined his surroundings, pausing to glance at a large collection of family photos arranged on a side table. 'There's a lot of children in your family,' he commented.

Topsy breathed in deep. 'Dante?' He swung round, stunning green eyes locking to her with sudden unexpected intensity, the power of his compelling attraction washing over her like a potent drug. 'Will you please tell me what you're doing here in London?'

'I *had* to see you,' he declared.

'But we have absolutely nothing to say to each other,' she reasoned in a voice strung tight with the strain of self-discipline.

'I care about you, Topsy,' he breathed thickly.

'Well, you have a funny way of showing it,' Topsy told him, unimpressed, indeed resenting that statement when his lack of concern for her feelings had been paraded in front of her at the ball. 'Until tonight I don't believe you've ever told me anything really personal about yourself. I even had to find out that you were once married from your mother. We had fun as you once said but it stopped being fun and I want out...*I am out.*'

His spectacular bone structure was rigid below his bronzed skin. 'When I mentioned my father tonight, it was to lessen your discomfort over your mother's arrest. I'm not used to talking about myself. I'm not used to sharing private matters with people.'

'Which only underlines how right I was to walk away.'

'But I'm not the *only* one of us who chose to keep secrets,' Dante countered suddenly, his green eyes ablaze with sudden condemnation.

'And what's that supposed to mean?' Topsy said defensively.

Dante pulled a small envelope from his pocket and extended it to her. 'Perhaps this will explain.'

Brow indenting, Topsy grasped the envelope. It felt like a greetings card but it wasn't her birthday. She tore it open to extract the card and flick it open.

Welcome to the family. Vittore.

Dante crossed the room to look over her shoulder and read the same message.

'What does he mean?' Topsy whispered, afraid

to believe that those words meant what she hoped they meant.

'The DNA tests were a match…' He skimmed her with a cool telling scrutiny. 'Yes, Vittore told me that you thought he might be your father but that you only approached him the night of the ball. Were you ever planning on sharing that possibility with me?'

Topsy was reeling, both from the news that the DNA testing had confirmed that Vittore was indeed her father and the wording of the card that seemed to offer to include her in the family circle. It seemed too good to be true. 'How does Vittore feel about it?'

'Since he's had a couple of days to absorb the shock of your existence, he seems pleased. He's also broken the news to my mother. She was certainly disconcerted when he explained about his unfortunate experience with your mother years ago, but *my* mother seems to have spent every moment since finding delightfully sentimental comparisons between you and her husband,' Dante revealed with an edge of derision.

'She says you have the same smile. Frankly I've never noticed.'

'I'm so glad your mother's not been distressed by all this coming out,' Topsy commented breathlessly. 'And of course you won't recognise any similarity in smiles when Vittore so rarely smiles around you. Why *would* he smile? Do you expect him to bask in your disapproval?'

'You realise this makes you my stepsister?' Dante prompted with a sardonic twist of his handsome mouth, ignoring her admonition with regard to his attitude towards his stepfather. 'And that the child my mother carries will be a half-sibling to *both* of us?'

Topsy smiled, thinking that over, and nodded. 'You have no idea what it's like not to know who your father is, particularly when your mother is as uninterested as Odette. Finding out the truth meant a lot to me, and Vittore and your mother are handling this in such a positive way. I'm very, very lucky,' she conceded gratefully.

'The information you required from your mother that persuaded you to work as an escort for an evening,' Dante recounted in a flat tone that could not hide his disapproval. 'Was that information the name of your father?'

'Yes,' Topsy confirmed, hating the fact that for the first time they were talking almost like polite strangers. Yet she wondered what other relationship they could possibly hope to establish in the wake of their unfortunate fling. At the same time she knew she would have to work on her own feelings because Vittore was her real father and Dante would always be a part of Vittore and Sofia's life.

In pursuit of that objective, she added in a rush, 'I grew up believing that another man, who lived abroad, was my father. I only met him a couple of times but when I was eighteen I discovered that he wasn't my father at all.'

'And finding out who was was *so* important to you that you took a job with my mother...for precisely what purpose?' Dante prompted tautly.

'I wanted the chance to get to know Vittore a little before I decided whether or not to approach him and then everything got so complicated.'

She sighed with a wry roll of her big dark eyes. 'Before I came to Italy I hadn't thought anything through. I saw the job offer on the castle website and decided it was a heaven-sent opportunity. But once I arrived, there they were—Sofia and Vittore, a newly married happy couple—and I was scared that if I did turn out to be Vittore's daughter, it would damage their marriage.'

'It could have done,' Dante conceded reflectively. 'Fortunately my mother isn't threatened by the discovery that her husband has an adult daughter but probably more important in this case is the fact that she already likes you, so you're not an unknown quantity she is being forced to accept.'

'Your mother's still been very generous,' Topsy responded.

'But I was quite right to be suspicious of your motives in coming to work for her. You accuse me of keeping secrets but really you kept many more secrets from all of us,' Dante condemned grimly. 'You came into my home and earned my mother's trust on false pretences.'

'That's not a fair criticism,' Topsy objected sharply.

'You know it is. I can understand the reasoning behind your masquerade but you also concealed who your family were and any hint that you were from a privileged background.'

Topsy flushed because that was more or less a true charge. 'I wasn't born into a privileged background. In fact there was nothing privileged about my life until Kat met Mikhail and married him. That was when everything changed and suddenly I was staying in a country mansion with servants at the weekends and Kat was buying me designer jeans.'

Someone rapped on the door of the lounge and Dante went to answer it.

'Would you like coffee?' Dante enquired over his shoulder. 'Or anything to eat?'

'No, thanks.' She didn't think she could get any sort of a drink past her tight throat and she was angry that Dante had put *her* on the defensive by reminding her that she had been downright dishonest when she deliberately took a job working for his mother simply to get close to Vittore. The acknowledgement embarrassed her. She hadn't set out to hurt anyone and, luckily, nobody had been hurt and surely that should be the bottom line that judged her behaviour.

'I wasn't honest about my family circumstances because I didn't want anyone questioning why I should need the job in the first place. I was also trying to take a break from my sisters and their expectations for a while and be independent,' she explained unwillingly, watching an ebony brow quirk. 'I love them all but they do meddle a lot in my life. I've never been allowed to make my own decisions. My sisters made the decisions for me, right down to who I dated and who I didn't date.'

'I wouldn't have even got on the list of potentials,' Dante quipped.

'Don't kid yourself, Dante.' Topsy wrinkled her slightly snub nose. 'You're rich and successful and those are exactly the qualities my sisters and their husbands respect.'

'Kusnirovich knows who I am and he was

ready to throw me out of his house tonight,' Dante observed grimly, his passionate mouth tightening into a hard line. 'There was neither respect nor acceptance in my reception. In all fairness, you're misjudging your family, *cara mia*. The instant you accused me of having another woman, it didn't matter *who* I was or *what* I was worth, they didn't want me anywhere near you.'

Topsy could see the truth of that for herself and her shoulders drooped, emotional exhaustion settling in as she sank down wearily on a well-padded sofa, allowing her rigid spine to sink into the cushions. 'I was tired of my family watching my every move, trying to fix me up with a job they picked, and that was another reason to come to Italy, except Mikhail tracked me down there as well.'

'They care about you,' Dante reasoned, oddly hesitant in his delivery, his accent purring along every syllable. 'As do I.'

Topsy froze, her small face rigid. 'I don't want to talk about Cosima. I still don't know what you're even doing here. Are you in London on business?'

'No. I'm here solely to see you,' Dante delivered.

'Why did you get married at twenty-one?' she asked him abruptly, determined to steer him off that subject lest it upset her and she let herself down by getting emotional. Attack, she thought, was the best part of defence. 'And why did you never mention that you had been married?'

Dante was palpably disconcerted by her reference to his being a widower and he breathed in deeply, as if he was bracing himself. 'To say the least, my life as a child and adolescent was dysfunctional. I thought that if I married young I could do it all differently and create the happy home I had never known. I also thought I loved Emilia. I never refer to my marriage because I made a mistake and I still feel guilty about that.' Dante virtually grated that final hard-edged admission. 'Are you satisfied now?'

'Satisfied with what? You're still not telling me what happened.'

'Emilia died, running across a busy road to meet me for lunch. While I was waiting for her… *before* I learned what had happened,' Dante framed jerkily, 'I was wishing she would at least leave me alone during working hours… That's how lousy a husband I was.'

Topsy was frowning, taken aback. 'You didn't love her?'

'I thought I did but with mature hindsight I think it was more a fond friendship on my side than love. Her parents had divorced. We both wanted a stable home life but she wanted too much of me and I felt suffocated, *trapped*,' he explained roughly, guiltily.

'How did she want too much of you?'

'If I wasn't with her she was phoning me constantly and she couldn't stand me leaving her to work. It was as though I had no right to a life of my own any more, but as far as Emilia was concerned that was how you loved someone. It didn't work for me; it was like living in a cage. I knew I shouldn't have married her within weeks.

I realised we were too different but I could never have hurt her by telling her that.'

'It's not your fault that she died,' Topsy told him gently.

'I know that…but I wasn't the best husband while she was alive. I was too young and self-ish and she was too needy,' he confided tight-mouthed. 'But there's nothing I can do about that now.'

He had regrets and Topsy was appalled to feel a dart of jealousy piercing her even on poor Emilia's behalf because she could not bear to picture Dante having been married to anyone.

'So, after that experience you didn't do seri-ous in relationships,' Topsy guessed.

'I didn't think I was cut out for serious after Emilia and I went for variety rather than qual-ity,' Dante acknowledged, his face forbidding in its detachment as though he seriously loathed having to tell her such a thing.

'There's no shame in avoiding what doesn't suit you,' Topsy mumbled abstractedly. 'We're all different—we're not meant to be the same. I've never done serious with anyone.'

Dante shot her a literal stabbing glance from glittering green eyes. 'I thought what we had *was* serious.'

'Which just goes to show how mistaken you can be,' Topsy parried with a strangled little laugh.

'Stop being so obstinate and listen to me!' Dante growled at her out of all patience, his eyes flashing with angry hostility. 'I was paired up with Cosima by her agent! She was not my girl-friend or my mistress or my lover or anything. She was chosen to publicise the ball and per-suade other celebrities that the event was fash-ionable enough for them to attend. We went out to dinner twice and attended a couple of par-ties to make it appear to the press that we were a couple. It is not an uncommon arrangement when good PR is required...'

Topsy was staring fixedly at him. 'You mean the hottest society couple in Italy was a fake romance? A show-mance?' she whispered shakily. '*Totally* fake?'

'Totally fake,' Dante confirmed. 'There was… er…a casual relationship with someone else at the time but that was over before I even met you.'

'But the way Cosima spoke to you at the ball…about your "agreement". What was that all about?' Topsy persisted, frowning, afraid to believe what he was telling her.

'I explained that I had met someone who would also be at the ball and she threw a fit at the threat of the paparazzi realising that I had lost interest in her and then assuming that she had been dumped. And Cosima naturally doesn't do dumped as part of her glossy image. She refused to come to the ball until I promised that I would maintain the act of being with her all evening and have nothing to do with any other woman,' he explained heavily. 'If I had had any idea how much grief that promise would cause me, I would never have agreed. But, at least, she turned up and gave the fund the publicity we needed for it.'

'But you *must* have fancied her,' Topsy breathed before she could think better of it. 'I mean, come on, Dante. Cosima's gorgeous and she's got a title like you, and even I have to admit that you look very well together.'

'No, I didn't fancy her in the slightest and she was very irritating company, talks about nothing but fashion and cosmetics,' Dante complained sardonically. 'At one point she called me a dinosaur for not being a fan of guy-liner.'

Topsy was surprised to find herself on the brink of laughing at the thought of that conversation. 'Let's face it, you are kind of conservative.'

'Please tell me you don't want me to wear guy-liner,' Dante urged, almost making that pent-up laughter bubble over inside her. 'I will do almost anything to get you back but I won't use make-up.'

'You don't need guy-liner. You've got great eyelashes,' she told him comfortingly.

Her brain had, however, leapt into a frantic whirl of excited and not particularly logical thoughts. He wanted her back. She wanted him back. For the first time that week the sick, tight feeling of isolation and loss had eased its stranglehold. He said he was serious about her. Could she believe that? Take the risk that he might respond to her feelings for him and give him another chance? But even through the chaos of her over-excited thoughts, there was one question she still had to ask and it was an obvious one.

'So, why didn't you tell me about your arrangement with Cosima *before* the ball?' Topsy asked doggedly, and as his gaze cloaked she immediately saw that it was a question he had hoped she wouldn't ask him.

'I hadn't quite worked out where you and I were going and making a big explanation about Cosima struck me as unnecessarily dramatic,' he advanced with visible reluctance.

'Unnecessarily dramatic?' Topsy yelled, jumping upright, a flush of frustrated fury colouring her heart-shaped face. 'How on earth could it be *unnecessarily dramatic* to explain about Cosima when you were sleeping in my bed with me every night?'

Dante shifted his feet restively, turned away, turned agitatedly back. 'I felt that it would be like making a big statement about our relationship and I was already uneasy about the way I was behaving with you.'

'A big statement,' Topsy repeated, unimpressed by that excuse. 'Why...*uneasy*?'

A deeply pained expression crossed his face. 'Do we have to discuss this now?'

'Yes, we do.' Topsy was sticking to her guns, recognising that she was in a much stronger position than she had appreciated.

'Even that I got involved with you in the first place was unusual for me. You were living in my home and I have never before developed an uncontrollable desire to ravish one of the staff. That felt weird,' Dante recounted flatly. 'And then I was staying with you every night, *all* night and that felt even weirder because I never hang around after sex.'

'My goodness, I was getting a treat and I didn't

even know it!' Topsy fired back with spirit. 'What was so weird about being attracted to me?'

'I thought you weren't my type but you're so much my type it's ridiculous,' Dante confessed and, without warning, suddenly stalked forward to reach for her hands with both of his. 'Please tell me that you're willing to move to Italy and live with me for ever, *gioia mia.*'

Topsy's eyes opened very wide indeed, her astonishment at that rapid turnaround unconcealed. 'That's a bit of a tall order, Dante. *For ever?*' she questioned weakly.

'Nothing less than for ever will do and I've already asked your father for his permission.'

'Permission for what?' she echoed.

And Dante got down on one knee in front of her, altogether depriving her of breath and voice, and extended a glittering diamond ring. 'Will you marry me?'

Topsy was so shattered by the marriage proposal that she crumpled back down on the edge of the sofa again. 'You're not serious...you can't be?'

'Why can't I be?' Dante demanded almost aggressively.

'You said you didn't do serious… I mean, you were really clear about that.'

'And then I met you…' A hand braced on her denim-clad thigh like a brand. 'And I fell insanely in love with you so fast I didn't know what was happening to me.'

'But you thought all those bad things about me…that I was chasing Vittore, that I was a regular escort girl.'

'And then you seduced me at the picnic,' Dante slotted in, green eyes glowing with sudden amusement.

'*I* seduced *you*?' Topsy gasped.

'You knew I couldn't keep my hands off you. Letting me take you somewhere that private wasn't a wise move,' Dante reasoned, quietly lifting her left hand and threading the diamond ring onto her engagement finger with a level of satisfaction he couldn't hide.

'But I didn't say yes yet!' Topsy protested. 'I

may be in love with you but it's too soon to talk about marriage.'

His hands curved to her cheeks and he leant forward to extract a hungry, demanding kiss that sent the blood crashing through her veins like a tidal wave as her pulses speeded up.

'You can stay the night,' she told him on the back of an ecstatic sigh.

'Not without a yes to the proposal. You get me back in bed only with a wedding ring,' Dante informed her combatively.

'You're the same man who just told me that marriage made you feel suffocated and trapped.'

'I'm not the same person I was a decade ago. You're not the needy, clingy type either. I can see you working away at a whiteboard in maths research and forgetting I even exist for hours at a stretch!' Dante confessed ruefully.

Topsy knew her own flaws. 'That is a possibility and you're right, I'm not clingy, but I still think it's too soon to be talking about marriage.'

'Without you in my life, I'll get stuffy and ruthless.'

'You're already ruthless and more stubborn than any man should be. You almost lost me because you wouldn't admit what you were feeling for me,' Topsy pointed out while she tangled her fingers lazily in his black hair in a caressing move that might have warned him that losing her was becoming increasingly unlikely.

'I love you,' Dante confided with breathtaking sincerity. 'And it makes me feel insecure. I won't be happy until you tell me that you'll marry me and stay with me for ever.'

Her amber eyes danced. 'The more you talk, the more I'm warming up to the prospect.'

'Do you want to stay here tonight or go back to my hotel with me?' Dante's hands were sliding up and down her slim thighs, rousing tingling heat in dangerous places.

'I think I might ravish you in the car if we leave,' Topsy admitted shakily.

'How do I match up to your list of required male characteristics?' Dante prompted, gathering her up into his arms with great care and tenderness.

'The truth? You don't match at all but you have other more important attributes,' Topsy whispered, smoothing a possessive hand over a high cheekbone that shifted down into a strong jawline. 'You love me. I love you, Dante Leonetti. Now let's go and find a guestroom for two.'

'And you'll marry me?' Dante pressed stubbornly.

'Well, I'm certainly not letting you go,' Topsy laughed, admiring the glitter of her ring in the lamplight.

'I couldn't bear to let you go,' he groaned, tightening his arms appreciatively round her. 'I love you so much I want you on a for ever and ever lease, *amata mia*.'

Topsy gave him a sunny smile, happiness darting and dancing through her like sunlight in the wake of a long winter. 'Oh, I think that can be arranged at no extra cost,' she teased.

EPILOGUE

TOPSY RACED OUT of the research department of the University of Florence, frantically checking her watch. She was late, she was always late, and sometimes it drove Dante, who was punctual to a fault, crazy.

Her husband awaited her in the car park, tall, dark and so breathtakingly handsome that not a female head in his vicinity failed to turn and look in his direction while his entire attention remained pinned to his windblown wife, half in and half out of her coat. He was lounging with folded arms and an air of long-suffering fortitude against the bonnet of his pristine Pagani Zonda.

'Do you know how fine you're cutting this, Dr Leonetti?' he demanded ruefully, beautiful green eyes tracking over her brightly smiling face with a love he couldn't and never tried to hide.

'I just got tied up with something.'

Dante opened the door for her and she slid in, smoothing her tunic top over the very small bump beneath.

'It's very important that you don't miss any appointments,' Dante told her anxiously. 'I want you to have the best possible care and attention.'

'Shut up,' his wife told him, lurching awkwardly into his lap before he could start the engine and kissing him breathless. 'I'm as healthy as a horse and I come from good breeding stock as well. How many nephews and nieces do I have?'

Dante, who had loosened up in his habits since Topsy came into his life, wrapped both arms around her and sighed into her tumbled dark hair. 'I know, but I can't take your casual attitude and I couldn't stand anything to happen to you.'

'It's *you* things are going to happen to!' Topsy warned him cheerfully. 'You're going to have me *and* a mini-me to torment you. Life as you know it has ended.'

'Life as I knew it ended the day I met you, *amata mia*,' Dante retorted with a wide smile of satisfaction, settling her back into the passenger seat and doing up her belt for her. 'Have you ever heard me complain?'

And Topsy had to admit, she had not heard him utter a single complaint in the three years since she had come to live in Italy. She had insisted on a long engagement and, regardless of Dante's eagerness to get to the altar, it was a year before the wedding actually took place. Topsy had wanted both of them to be absolutely certain of what they were doing because she really did want their marriage to last for ever and ever.

Deciding to try for a baby had been a big decision and she had waited until she was twenty-six to do so, confident that she would be a more caring parent than her mother had been and convinced that Dante would make a terrific father. It had been something of a shock when she fell pregnant the first month but she was truly excited about her baby.

She had had no difficulty finding a research job at the university and was currently up for an award following the publication of her most recent maths paper. Her career took up a good deal of her time and she was frequently invited abroad to speak and share her research, as well as continually fending off head-hunters desperate to employ her in more profit-inspired fields. Dante had not been able to tolerate living away from her during the week to be at the bank headquarters in Milan. Nowadays, although he made regular business trips, he mostly worked from home.

The fancy-dress ball that had caused so much trouble between them was now a more positive memory for them both for the little girl suffering from leukaemia had travelled to the USA for highly specialised treatment and was now in recovery with every hope of maintaining her improved health.

On a less important note, Topsy still couldn't

drive, had decided she didn't like driving and flatly refused to get behind a steering wheel with Dante beside her but it wasn't really a big problem when Dante had hired a local driver to motor her around instead.

Vittore and Sofia and little Agnese, their daughter, who was now a cherubic toddler, had moved into their new home, Casa di Fortuna. Family contact was frequent and informal and everything that Topsy had learned to enjoy with her sister and their families. Kat had given birth safely to her much-longed-for little daughter. Topsy's relationship with her father was open and affectionate and more than she had ever hoped to have with a parent. Dante had learned to recognise Vittore's deep love for his mother and the awkwardness between the two men had slowly melted away.

Sadly, but not surprisingly, nothing had changed about Topsy's relationship with her mother. Odette had been tried in court and had got off the charges through lack of acceptable proof, but the older woman's jubilation had not lasted long when she realised that all her regular clients had deserted her because they had feared exposure after her arrest. In the end, Odette had closed down the escort agency and retired to the South of France to live on the pension she received from her sons-in-law. Neither Topsy nor any of her sisters had heard from Odette since she had relocated abroad two years earlier and, as the older woman had not written the tell-all book she had threatened to write, her daughters were inclined to think that silence from their mother was a blessing.

'There…we just made it,' Dante pronounced with a touch of superiority as he shot the car into a parking spot beside the obstetrician's consulting rooms.

'I knew we would,' Topsy teased, tenderly stroking the back of a lean brown hand where it still rested on the steering wheel. 'You would hate to miss a scan of our daughter.'

Dante tucked a straying strand of dark hair gently back behind her ear, his reflective green gaze resting warmly on her animated face. 'I never knew I could be so happy…and just to think there's going to be *two* of you. I can't believe my luck, *amata mia.*'

Topsy gave him a knowing look that engulfed him in love. 'I believe we make our own luck.'

* * * * *

Mills & Boon® Large Print

January 2014

CHALLENGING DANTE
Lynne Graham

CAPTIVATED BY HER INNOCENCE
Kim Lawrence

LOST TO THE DESERT WARRIOR
Sarah Morgan

HIS UNEXPECTED LEGACY
Chantelle Shaw

NEVER SAY NO TO A CAFFARELLI
Melanie Milburne

HIS RING IS NOT ENOUGH
Maisey Yates

A REPUTATION TO UPHOLD
Victoria Parker

BOUND BY A BABY
Kate Hardy

IN THE LINE OF DUTY
Ami Weaver

PATCHWORK FAMILY IN THE OUTBACK
Soraya Lane

THE REBOUND GUY
Fiona Harper

Mills & Boon® Large Print
February 2014

THE GREEK'S MARRIAGE BARGAIN
Sharon Kendrick

AN ENTICING DEBT TO PAY
Annie West

THE PLAYBOY OF PUERTO BANÚS
Carol Marinelli

MARRIAGE MADE OF SECRETS
Maya Blake

NEVER UNDERESTIMATE A CAFFARELLI
Melanie Milburne

THE DIVORCE PARTY
Jennifer Hayward

A HINT OF SCANDAL
Tara Pammi

SINGLE DAD'S CHRISTMAS MIRACLE
Susan Meier

SNOWBOUND WITH THE SOLDIER
Jennifer Faye

THE REDEMPTION OF RICO D'ANGELO
Michelle Douglas

BLAME IT ON THE CHAMPAGNE
Nina Harrington

Rom LP